For David,
Look out for the feathers for your
journey; hold tight;
Gregory Maguire
Dec 1982

LIGHTS *on the* LAKE

Also by Gregory Maguire

THE LIGHTNING TIME

THE DAUGHTER OF THE MOON

LIGHTS
on the
LAKE

Gregory Maguire

Farrar · Straus · Giroux

New York

The epigraph, from *The Lyman Letters,* by Richard B.
Sewall (Amherst, Mass.: The University of Massachusetts
Press, 1965), appears courtesy of the President and
Fellows of Harvard University

Library of Congress Cataloging in Publication Data
Maguire, Gregory. Lights on the lake.
[1. Death—Fiction. 2. Adirondack Mountains (N.Y.)—
Fiction. 3. Fantasy] I. Title.
PZ7.M2762Lk 1981 [Fic] 81-12478
ISBN 0-374-34463-9 AACR2

FOR ROGER MOCK

*"So I conclude that space & time
are things of the body & have little
or nothing to do with our selves . . ."*
—Emily Dickinson

LIGHTS *on the* LAKE

Prologue

If a bird had come racking its wings in the icy air over the lake, it might have seen a boy skimming along the road with the speed of one pursued. Scarf trailing, arms and legs pumping, black boots thumping on the black-topped road. The sound of those thumping boots wouldn't travel very far; the wind was high and noisy. But a bird sailing in over the frozen lake might notice the steady course and unflagging pace of the young runner.

His head was bare, and wind and running blew his hair back off his forehead. A knit ski cap was balled in one fist, and a green knapsack had slipped untidily under his other arm. He didn't stop to adjust it.

Any bird wheeling over the dormers and chimneys of the big white house, looking perhaps for the bread crusts occasionally scattered in the snowy yard, might be frightened by the commotion in the front of the house. Might alight on the peak of the roof to await the calm necessary for scavenging. Might watch.

The boy was slogging down the ice-rutted driveway toward the small front porch, where a middle-aged woman in a fur coat and a mustached young man wearing a black shirtfront with a bit of white collar showing were struggling with luggage. The boy threw himself into service at once, grabbing a sleeping bag. The woman made a lot of noise and pointed to her wrist repeatedly. The young man tried to squeeze a suitcase under his one arm and a canvas satchel and a flute case under his other. The suitcase flopped open, spilling underwear and socks and shaving supplies into the snow.

The woman covered her eyes. The young man struggled and grinned. The boy threw the sleeping bag into the car and ran back to grab at the clothes, shaking drops of snow off them, trying to stuff them into the suitcase again. The young man and the boy were laughing; the suitcase energetically resisted being reclosed. The two of them finally had to kneel on it, the young man slapping the bright clasps.

The woman got into a station wagon and started the motor. This prompted the young man to pile the luggage indecorously into the back. He turned then to speak to the boy.

But other people came out of the house: a woman in an apron, a man in overalls, another man in another black shirtfront with a white collar. Suddenly the people were hugging the young man, as the woman in the car gunned the motor. Lots of squealing laughter, flailing arms around each other.

A cautious bird would be watching every move. So much activity could mean danger. Only the boy was still, intently inspecting the knit ski cap in his hands, till the young man came up to him, clasped him on the shoulder, and said something funny, which made them both laugh.

Then there was a space at the end of the laugh when no one said anything. Then the young man got in the car and the woman drove it away, and slowly the others stopped waving and went back into the house. Only the boy was left, waving long after the car was out of sight. A bird on the rooftop might have been able to watch the car a long way down the road, but to the solitary boy in the driveway, it was quite gone.

It would have been only a short interruption to a hungry bird, a ten-minute delay to feeding time. The yard was quiet now. It would be safe to swoop down and feed on the stiff rye crusts and charred toast crumbs. That single boy was too still to be much threat. Coming down to the snow-covered lawn, so close, a bird at last might have been able to see a look of bewildered loneliness settling heavily on the boy's features—but what kind of bird would be so perceptive as to notice that?

Chapter One

Taking their time, two adults were hobbling up the icy walk. No, not hobbling, bumping. The fattish woman was bumping and dragging the slender man. She looked angry. He looked nothing.

Maybe, thought Daniel, watching from inside the front door, they were coming for ashes and knew they were late. He had never seen them before, but Ash Wednesday made some people go to church who usually stayed home.

"Damn," said the woman.

They haven't come for ashes, Daniel decided, opening the front door.

"This the Myer House?" Her voice scratched at Daniel.

"Yes," he said.

"Bring the knapsack and guitar from the back seat, like a good boy. Grab the shopping bag with the dirty laundry in it, too. I didn't have time to run to the laundromat."

"I'll call Mrs. Phalen," said Daniel. The woman was settling the thin young man on the porch railing. Daniel rang the doorbell briskly—it was a real bell, with a ribbon tied to its rusting clapper—and then he ran obediently to the small car, whose doors were flapped open to the cold.

He gathered things and stumbled back, passing the woman on the walk.

The man was leaning against the porch pillar, eyes closed.

"Mrs. Phalen?" called Daniel. When the housekeeper didn't appear, Daniel remembered that she was still in chapel tidying up after the Ash Wednesday service.

"She's—uh—there's nobody in the house right now," he said.

"Suits me just fine," said the woman shortly, hauling a cardboard carton out of the back seat.

"Should I run and get her?"

"No, this'll just be a minute." The woman dropped the carton on the porch; the top flapped open and a book bounced out into the snow. Daniel lunged after it, glad for something to do.

"Don't break your back over a book, kiddo. Books are one thing he's not shy of."

The man leaning up against the pillar swallowed and steadied himself, as if he'd just staggered off a merry-go-round. He looked as if he didn't quite know what was going on. That's just how I feel, thought Daniel, and rang the bell for Mrs. Phalen again.

"Stop the hullabaloo," said the woman. She knelt down on the stone steps and fished through the knapsack. "This is a friend of your priest Petrakis. There's a letter in here inviting him to come visit, and so he's come. I can't do anything with him anymore and won't be made to. I'm not going to put up with this one's stares and silences. I've got kids and a house that needs looking after. A brother is a dispensable item, if you ask me. So your priest Petrakis can look after him."

I'm only a visitor at the Myer House, I don't live here; it was just an accident that I was here when you people came, thought Daniel nervously. I don't have any say in who comes or goes; you're talking to me as if I'm in charge.

"Father Petrakis is away for a time." He tried not to sound timid. "Can I ask you your name?"

"Filoretti O'Toole." The woman found a piece of paper and thrust it at Daniel. "But it won't do you any good to call. My Bob's had enough. And it's not our responsibility."

Daniel looked at the thin young man. His face was white as the snow on the railings.

"Is this your brother?" he said.

Filoretti O'Toole was searching her pockets for her car keys. "I can't see the reason for brothers and sisters hanging on each other. I've had it with him, up to here, do you get it?"

Daniel thought of his own sister, who was grown up and married, and he suddenly got angry. "What's wrong with people taking care of each other, even when they're older?"

"Who's got the time for it? If you do, you drag that guy inside and tend to him." She opened her car door.

The young man suddenly looked as if he was going to pass out.

"You're not going to just *leave* him here? Father Petrakis is in New Mexico!" Daniel ran down to the side of the car. "He left an hour ago."

"So you do the Good Samaritan act." Filoretti O'Toole climbed in behind the wheel and started the engine, staring straight ahead of her. "I don't want him, I tell you."

"You don't WANT him? But he's your BROTHER!" shouted Daniel over the engine's noise, and then the car careered out the driveway, back onto Route 103.

The exhaust from the car faded in the cold air; the slanting winter sunlight threw long shadows across the snowy lawn. When Daniel turned back to the house, he found that Filoretti's brother had slumped to the floor of the porch in a daze.

"MRS. PHALEN!" yelled Daniel, and kicked open the storm door and tried to drag the young man over the threshold into the front hall of the Myer House.

"Daniel Rider, what in the world are you doing to that man?" Martha Phalen finally came rushing into the front hall, her sleeves rolled up past her elbows and a stack of hymnals in her arms. She dropped them on the telephone table and fell to her knees next to the young man. "What have you done to him?"

"I didn't do anything but pull him inside. His sister left him on the doorstep like a baby in a basket."

"You've no call to be opening the door to strangers, Daniel, you should have run and got me from chapel. Young man, get up. What's your name?"

"I *called* you and I rang the bell. She was furious, Mrs. Phalen, she just wanted to get rid of him," said Daniel.

"Oh, Father Marston's going to like this one. I can hear it already, and it's not nice. Daniel, why did you open the door to her? What's wrong with this guy?"

"Because she was so mean. And he's sick, I think. Look at him."

Mrs. Phalen stood up. "Well, you'll have to answer to Father Marston on this one, Daniel. It's a little bold of you to go dragging people in off the doorstep. I'll call Dr. Fell."

"He's a friend of Father August's. That's what she said. Here's a letter about it she gave me."

Mrs. Phalen dialed the phone, drumming her fingers on the pile of red hymnals. "Go get Sam, in the woodshed," she said to Daniel suddenly, "so we can get this guy onto a sofa. Hello, this is Martha Phalen at the Myer House—"

Sam Phalen came, and he and his wife carried the young man into the front room.

Daniel lugged the knapsack and guitar and the box of books into the front hall, and he wondered whether to follow the Phalens into the front room. While he was waiting, and listening, and trying to tell by the sounds and the whispers what was going on, he looked at the book that had fallen in the snow. It was a paperback volume of poetry, called *Nineteen Degrees East*. And it was by Nikos Griskas. The photograph on the back was a picture of the young man who right now was stretched out in the front room of the Myer House.

Daniel set the book down carefully on the step next to him. Nikos Griskas, a poet, a friend of Father August's. What would this tired guy say when he realized that Father August had gone away for six weeks? Would he be miserable? Angry? Feel rejected?

There was some misery and maybe some anger in the back of Daniel's own thoughts. He had raced out of school, not waiting for the school bus because it went the long way around the lake, ignoring his classmates, who were ignoring him, and he'd run non-stop all the way to the Myer House so he could bid his friend Father August goodbye. He'd said goodbye yesterday, a preliminary one, but it hadn't really counted, and August had said they'd see each other today before he left.

But when Daniel had arrived, August had been nearly ready to go. There'd been people around; Mrs. Tyne, who was driving him to the airport in Albany so he could catch a plane to the Southwest, and then Sam and Martha Phalen, and Father Marston. There'd been a lot of noise and confusion, no private time. August must have been excited about going, anxious about missing his flight. With the distractions of the moment, he'd had little attention to give to Daniel.

Some friend, thought Daniel, his mouth dry with bad feeling. Says he'll see you one last time and then it's all of two minutes long. The things Daniel had been saving up to say, about hoping he had a good time, about asking him to send a postcard, to listen for coyotes, to *remember* him, were all left useless in some space between the back of his tongue and his brain.

When Nikos Griskas came to and found August had gone away for six weeks, would he also feel so abandoned? Forgotten? We could start a club, thought Daniel, and call it the leftovers. The left-behinds.

Dr. Fell came about an hour later. Daniel was still hanging around. Dr. Fell had a clarion voice and an uncompromising manner. "Nothing wrong with this one," he announced twenty minutes after he arrived. His voice rang through the closed doors. Daniel strained for the Phalens' reaction, but it was inaudible.

"Look, Mrs. Phalen, you can listen through my stethoscope, or feel for the pulse as well as I can," the doctor was saying irritably. "Blood pressure—normal. Pulse— normal. Temperature—normal. Now, what do you want from me?"

There was a slow, muffled statement from Sam Phalen. Daniel moved as close to the door as he could.

"*I* don't know what you're to do. Call up that lady who said she was his sister. God knows, you're not responsible. He's in perfect health. Just another lazy kid."

"Thank you, Dr. Fell," said Martha Phalen, opening the door into the hall. "We'll take care of it from here."

"Toss him out. Nothing wrong with him that a little

fresh air won't cure," said Dr. Fell cheerfully. "Why, here's the Rider boy. Hello, Danny. How's your mother? Been taking her medicine?"

"I guess so. She seems fine." Daniel had sat down suddenly on the steps, to make it look as if he had been there for a while. He stared intently at a page of the book of Nikos's poems.

"Well, we can't throw him out in the snow." Mrs. Phalen folded her arms and watched Dr. Fell's car disappear. "Father Marston won't be home until tomorrow. And Father Petrakis won't be home for six weeks. But we can't just toss him out, no matter what Doc Fell says."

"Put him in the back bedroom, Martha," said Sam Phalen, heading back outside for the toolshed. "Maybe it's a spell of some kind and he'll come out of it."

Mrs. Phalen charged upstairs to get some fresh linen to make up a bed. Daniel stole to the door of the living room.

Nikos Griskas was stretched out on the sofa. His face was pale against the blue-green flowery upholstery. His eyes were open. His forehead was beaded with sweat.

"Hi," said Daniel softly.

Nikos didn't answer. His eyes didn't even blink at Daniel's words. He might have been dead, but for the faint intake of breath. He might have been asleep, but for his open eyes. He might at least have answered, thought Daniel, since I was friendly enough to say hello.

Mrs. Phalen came churning into the room. "Come on, Daniel, you offered him sanctuary, you can help me a bit now, too. Get on his other side." She put her arm around

Nikos's shoulders and began pulling him to his feet. Nikos swayed heavily between Mrs. Phalen and Daniel.

Somehow they managed to get Nikos up the stairs, and landed him in the back bedroom. Daniel could see Canaan Lake just outside the window, its surface ice-marble, its far shores lined with bare trees.

Mrs. Phalen began to unbutton Nikos's shirt. "Daniel, you can make yourself useful by grabbing a couple of towels from the bathroom closet." Daniel found two brown towels, and set them on the dresser, just beneath the wall crucifix.

"Who is he?"

Mrs. Phalen flapped a rough blanket over Nikos's prostrate form. "A friend of Father August's. I'm having trouble placing him exactly. He's been here before, I think. I recognize him, though he's thinner and gaunter than I remembered him. And that letter was from Father August, inviting him to come for a visit sometime. But even though both priests are out just now, I'll turn no sick man or woman from this door. Now, out of here." She was suddenly snappy. "I don't know why he's come, but he needs a little peace and quiet. You've been here since school let out, Daniel, why don't you go along now."

He was out the door before he remembered that he had stuffed *Nineteen Degrees East* in his coat pocket. So he opened it up. Its edges had curled from its contact with the snow earlier. The words sat blackly and squarely on the pages, with lots of white space like snowdrifts around them. A piece of notebook paper, with neat printing on it, fluttered out from the center of the book. It was a poem, dated early last month. At the top of the page: *Teacher.*

The congregation had disbanded long ago, and both the Phalens were busy with their work. Father Marston had sped away to a mission church somewhere for another Ash Wednesday service. No one was around. Daniel found the window that would be Nikos's, on the second floor of the Myer House. And Daniel read the poem out loud, half to the senseless Nikos and half to the fish that might be frozen alive in the ice of Canaan Lake.

> *I turn the world between my thumb and forefinger,*
> *Like a bauble on display, for sale.*
> *Look, the little oceans have their singular tides—*
> *And maybe little fishes, in perfect, infinitesimal*
>   *scale.*
>
> *And you do yet, and always will, extend*
> *As wide as galaxies, as long as time.*
> *Quadrants and quasars can't account for your*
>   *influence.*
> *A universe of meaning quelling time's dry judicial*
>   *voice.*
>
> *When meaning measures equal with the matter*
> *You will be found inherent in every sea and sun;*
> *And size will be dismissed, and learning shatter*
> *All my various walls, and this loneliness will be*
>   *done.*

Who is he talking about? What Teacher? God? This is a weird poem, thought Daniel. But Nikos is a weird person anyway, sick and not sick at the same time. Weird and unfortunate too, dumped here for Father August to take care of. Well, being left behind is one thing we have in common.

Daniel started shivering from the cold wind that drove in over the icy lake, so he shoved the poetry book back in his pocket and headed for home, the smudge of ashes still visible on his forehead.

Chapter Two

After school the next day, Daniel turned on the television. "Turn that off!" called his mother, from a floor and a half away.

"It's educational!" hoped Daniel at top voice.

A lot of people in old-fashioned costumes were talking about the New World, drawing a map of it based on the loud descriptions of a balding man who kept hitting people on the head with an American Indian peace pipe. Daniel couldn't figure out if it was supposed to be comical or informative. It didn't really seem like either. But it was better than staring out the window.

"Trash!" said Mrs. Rider from the doorway. "Turn it right off."

"Oh, Ma," said Daniel, obeying.

"New World, indeed. You ought to do your own discovery of a new world, Daniel; why don't you go out and play? Don't you have any friends from school yet that you can play with?"

"It's not as easy as you think," Daniel said testily. "They've all known each other since kindergarten. I'm a foreigner as far as they're concerned."

"Oh, Daniel, you have to try a little."

I do try. Daniel stared at the blank television screen. The world was gray like the television world sometimes; when he was at school he walked through the classes like a child actor in a television movie. He never really knew what he was feeling; he only knew that he was doing what he was supposed to be doing: lining up for dismissal, sharpening pencils, raising his hand to answer questions. He was behaving like a model student. But the model student was isolated in a noisy classroom of normal easy kids, all of whom had known each other for years and were relaxed about it. Nobody else had to act the part of being a child except him.

"Daniel, did you hear me?" Mrs. Rider was looking at him oddly.

Mr. Rider came to the door. "Marion, I had a legal-size pad of yellow paper with a page of notes I'd taken this morning on the phone with Charles Mooney. Do you know where it is?"

"Haven't seen it. I've been upstairs."

"Well, it's important. It contains the outlines of my April column for *National Reporter*. What's he doing in here?"

"Going out to play, I think."

"It's impossible to keep anything in this house. Daniel, have you seen it?"

"Nope."

"Don't use that slang. Marion, if this working at home is to be successful for me, you're going to have to become accustomed to my notetaking."

"I've been upstairs with the dusting. Did you look under the newspapers on the television table? I bet it's right there."

Mr. Rider went to look, grunting at finding it there, and then went back upstairs to the room he was using as an office for his political writing.

Daniel sank back into the chair, hoping his mother would have forgotten her mission with the interruption. His father had naturally missed the conversation between his mother and himself, befogged as usual with his own concerns. He could at least have asked how school was, thought Daniel. Or if I missed Father August. Or if I was happy being a leftover.

"Are you conking out in the middle of the afternoon?" said Mrs. Rider. "Come on, a little more spirit, Daniel."

"All right. Gotcha. Lemme outa here," said Daniel in what he hoped was a prisoner of war's desperate gravelly voice. And partly as a model child obeying his mother and partly as a boy resigned to the inevitability of such tiresome things, he grabbed his coat and his scarf and headed for the door.

"And if you're going to be walking past the Myer House," his mother called after him, "tell Father Marston I'll need to see the original contracts he signed with the Ogleson Brothers to see if they're violating their agreement on this repair work." Mrs. Rider, with her background in management and finance, was trying to straighten out the parish financial records, which had fallen into a terrible mess in recent years.

"I'll never remember that," said Daniel.

"*Original Ogleson contract*," said his mother. "Ten to one, they won't even be able to find it."

Daniel scuffed along Route 103, cracking the ice in the ditches by the road, kicking miniature blizzards off bushes. The sky was solid uninterrupted gray overhead, like a stretch of dull steel. The sky crowded him into the lake valley; it rested almost like a lid on the crests of the lower mountains around Canaan Lake.

As early as he could remember, he'd wanted to live in the country. Way back when he was five and six and seven, beginning to read for himself, the books he'd liked best had illustrations which showed people living in low, single-family houses. They could walk right out the door onto the grass, those people; they could fall out of the windows and not get killed. The world was right up close to them. But the Rider family had lived in an apartment four floors up, with the windows nailed shut, and Daniel hadn't even been able to see the treeless street below unless he stood on a chair and looked over the sill. He'd brought dozens of his messy watercolors home from school, showing houses with doors that led right out onto bright flower-strewn lawns, houses with windows low enough to climb into and fall out of, but his parents hadn't taken the hint.

Now here he was, eleven years of city life behind him, and this twelfth year unrolling in the isolated North Country of upstate New York, and he was more miserable than he'd ever been. At least in Manhattan there'd been people *around*. Here you had to walk a mile before you even ran into another soul.

He tried to laugh at his own misery. After all, it was still early. They'd only been living here in Canaan Lake for two months. Things took time. And it wasn't so bad. What made it hard was that when he had come the first time, at Thanksgiving, there had been Grandma and Father August Petrakis. Then Grandma had died, and now Father August was gone. And nobody at school seemed like a potential friend, so that left Daniel remorsefully alone, looking for someone to talk to.

So he trudged toward the Myer House. Mrs. Phalen's unyielding authority awed him, but his mother's request gave him a valid excuse for being there. And perhaps Nikos would be awake or alert today. It was something to do, at least. There was nothing else to do.

Vera Malecki Meister was in the kitchen, taking some tea with Mrs. Phalen. Only entertaining a guest would stop Mrs. Phalen's whirlwind of chores. Daniel sidled up to the swinging door to listen.

"But have you found out anything else, Martha? Lord knows, there's *something* wrong. I wouldn't trust Dr. Fell as far as I could throw him. In this matter, at least; once he gave me some very good pills for an ailment I had— but tell me more. Surely you've heard?—"

"He is Nikos Griskas," said Martha Phalen. "His sister lives in Glens Falls with her husband and five children. I called her last night to find out what's wrong with him. She hung up on me."

"Nikos Griskas . . ." Daniel could almost hear Vera Meister thinking. "Seems to me I've heard that name before . . ."

"Well, he's a friend of Father August's," said Mrs. Phalen.

"I know, you told me."

"And he's a poet, a published poet."

"Now I wouldn't know his name from reading any poetry books. I've hardly time for the newspaper and the parish bulletin. No, I've heard of him elsewhere . . . the name rings a bell."

"It was Daniel Rider, you know, who took him in. I'm not sure exactly what's going to happen. Father Marston wasn't entirely pleased with the whole event. I do hope Nikos recovers soon."

Daniel swallowed. He hoped so, too; the Myer House staff had to handle a problem that Daniel had accepted for them. If Nikos got better quickly, there'd be less blame on Daniel for welcoming him there.

Though what's blame got to do with it? he thought suddenly. The guy was sick, and his sister was throwing him out like an old pair of shoes! Daniel got warm with anger all over again.

"That name," muttered Vera. "Rings a bell, it does, it does."

Daniel waited. He could hear clinks and sips and hums as the two women relaxed in the kitchen. He decided he'd better go in and ask Mrs. Phalen if he could say hello to Nikos. Just as he pressed against the swinging door, Vera's voice rang out triumphantly: "Oh, preserve us, Martha, it was the Nesbitt thing! Last month!"

Both women's mouths were open and their eyes widened. They turned and gaped at Daniel in the doorway. Fish, he thought suddenly.

Then their mouths clamped closed. Daniel knew they wouldn't say another word in his presence. It was the way of the world. He didn't even mind.

"Hello. I've come to see if Nikos is still here," he said.

"Not fit for visitors, Daniel." Mrs. Phalen took a last gulp and stood up. "How did you know his name?"

"It was in a book that fell out of a box."

"Oh. Well. Some other time, perhaps."

"Is he awake?"

Vera smiled. "Marvelous, isn't it? 'Thou shalt love thy neighbor as thyself.' Daniel, you're such a considerate boy."

I'm bored and lonely, not considerate, thought Daniel.

"Now, Vera." Martha Phalen rinsed cups. "There's enough of the Good Book plastered on these walls as it is, no need for you to start."

"Well." Vera didn't mind the rebuke. She ran fingers along her wrinkled brow, as if trying to massage her memory. "Time to go, Martha. The boardinghouse business never lets up, even in the dead of winter."

"Accurate phrase for this kind of day," said Mrs. Phalen, juggling some onions out of a bag. "The dead of winter."

"And appropriate to your houseguest," said Vera ominously, delighting in her cleverness.

Daniel stared. Mrs. Phalen chopped the green tails off the onions. "On the other hand, Daniel, you might say hello," she said casually. "Just for a minute."

So Daniel had to leave, had to go upstairs and miss the conversation the two women would have about the dead of winter.

On the second floor, Father Marston's typewriter rattled along, clicking and ringing over Sunday's sermon. At least the vicar was occupied and wouldn't be likely to scold Daniel for his part in yesterday's drama.

Daniel turned into Father August's room, by habit, and was made lonelier by the emptiness there. It was neat, proper; it was nothing without its occupant.

In the spare room Daniel found Nikos, fully dressed, stretched out on the bed with his hands on his eyes. Books were flopped open to special pages, six or eight on the floor near the bed.

"I have another book for you." Daniel took *Nineteen Degrees East* out of his pocket.

Nikos uncovered his eyes. They were red and wet.

Daniel started to put the book down.

"Keep it." The young man's voice throttled in his throat.

"It's yours, though."

Nikos sat up and looked at Daniel. His hair, dark curls, ranged like black fire from his head, and fire was contained in those eyes, too. Eyes the color of ashes, gray-oak color. His whole body, sheathed in jeans and a plaid flannel shirt, twitched with some quiet violence. Daniel could feel the furnace heat across the room. He backed away, out the door, fast.

"A dreadful time," Vera was insisting to Mrs. Phalen, as Daniel sped past.

Outside, the February chill stilled the fever in Daniel. He plowed through the snow to the edge of the lake, and shivered and sneezed. Why was August Petrakis gone? Daniel hadn't known him long but he knew that August was different. He was made differently, his ears could hear meanings behind people's everyday words. He'd be able to understand what was making Nikos sick by looking at him, talking to him for a minute; Daniel was sure of it.

But, be sensible, Daniel said to himself, testing the ice on Canaan Lake with a tentative bôot. Nikos wasn't *really* burning. He just seemed—agitated—and it was contagious. He wasn't *really* giving off heat.

The ice held. Daniel moved out, a few feet from shore, walking in slow motion, all muscles tensed, breath suspended. Nothing cracked. He relaxed and started home.

What had Nikos done? Or what had happened? What was the Nesbitt thing that Vera Meister had remembered? Who would know?

Daniel glanced around the lakeshore, to remind himself of who lived here, to help him think of who might know. Nobody at the Myer House would tell him. And Vera wouldn't think it was fit for his youthful ears, either, judging by her tone. His parents didn't know the local gossip yet. And the postmistress, Eulalie Spencer, would take savage delight in withholding information.

On the other side of the lake were the Grobers' house, and old Adelaide Putney's, and the two Mrs. McDonalds'. Which of them would know, or tell him?

There was a fog on that shore, an afternoon mist. The lights in Grobers' and Miss Putney's were dimmed. Were gone.

Daniel stood still on the ice.

That was odd. There was no other mist, not on the northeast shore nor behind him on Route 103 nor back toward the town of Canaan Lake. Just there, on the northwest shore, a shimmering stretch of fog.

Daniel's heart suddenly pounded like a drum giving alarm. Something's happening, he thought, something inexplicable. So soon! He dug his fingernails into the frayed tips of his gloves. Daniel had seen impossible things before. He was excited and frightened at the same time.

But nothing happened. Slowly the fog, the strangely bright fog, disappeared, and the Grobers' lights shone palely again, sick yellow rectangles reflected in the ice.

There was nothing else for Daniel to do. He would probably be late for dinner and his mother would be angry. It couldn't be helped. He had to cross the lake, to see if the ice was cracked there, to see if the mist was only evaporated lakewater rising from a crack in the ice.

Water doesn't evaporate in this weather, Daniel told himself. Not great clouds of water, not in February, not misting water. But he had to be sure. He couldn't assume anything.

It took nearly an hour to get around to that side of the lake. He might have crossed over the ice, in a direct line, and taken only fifteen minutes, but he was scared of the ice and of its cracking. So he trudged all the way around the northwest shore and found the ice intact, completely solid to the edge of the lake, just as it had been over on his side.

He stared at the Grober house, memorizing its shape, the placement of windows in its clapboard side, so that he could make it out in the mist, if that funny mist came again.

He knew that it would.

"Looking for someone?"

A solid shape was traveling steadily toward him across the ice. It must have come out of the house on the other side of Grobers'.

"Oh. It's you." Susan Barrey, a girl in his class at school, set her hands on her hips and regarded him as if for the first time. "What are you doing on this side of the water?"

"I just came over to see something." Daniel wasn't inclined to share any mystery with Susan Barrey. He felt himself turning into the model boy: well-spoken, distant, polite.

"To see what? The great smoke?"

Daniel studied the roofline of the Barrey house. It was not a straight line; instead it sagged and lifted, interrupted by the fieldstone chimney in the middle. It was a makeshift roof, with missing slates and splotches of tar that someone had slopped around. Daniel observed all this carefully and said, "The great smoke?"

"Yeah. I saw you coming over—I thought maybe you saw the commotion. Thanks for coming. Everything's okay though."

"Good," said Daniel, working to involve her further, to get more out of her. "I was—concerned."

"You're nice." Susan Barrey smiled, and Daniel hoped she wasn't getting the wrong idea. "You're new around here, and yet you come by to see what was wrong. I appreciate that."

He had never heard her say so much at once. In school, Susan Barrey sat like a bored delegate at an overlong convention. Nothing as interesting as disdain or revulsion ever showed on her face. She handed assignments in on time, and got them back glowing with stars and red A's, and she looked as if she couldn't care less. In his two months at the new school, Daniel hadn't been able to guess a thing about her. But she neither approached nor avoided her classmates in friendship, which suggested some other, consuming interest.

"I can't stay out here, not with Papa all alone—care to come in?"

Why would Susan Barrey invite him into her house? Why would she be cordial and inviting now, when in school she wouldn't speak a word unless the teacher asked her something? Her reserve was so strong in school that its absence now made Daniel wary.

"Did you hear me? If you want to come in, then come in."

"Okay." And Daniel found himself knocking the snow off his boots and following Susan Barrey into the dark, square rooms of the old stone house where she lived.

"My grandfather did this. Not meaning to, of course." Susan opened a door, and the bitterness of burnt matter struck. The room was dense with stink. There was no visible smoke, but the air was dark and the surfaces of the furniture had absorbed a shade or two of dark. And in a sink a blackened frying pan was soaking.

"I just moved him to the front room," said Susan, "so I could open the windows without chilling him. And then I saw you out on the ice, looking. Here, would you open that back window?"

"It won't stay up."

"Prop it up with a spoon or something."

"What happened?"

"When the school bus left me off, I saw smoke in the house. Papa was trying to surprise me with dinner. He was frying eggs and he fell asleep. I thought the house was on fire at first, the smoke was dreadful. But it was just eggs and sausage. Papa is so upset."

"Where are your parents?"

Susan started scraping at the immersed pan with a fork, flaking off shingles of black. "Well. Away, for a time. Traveling in the South. They have a house down in Miami. I live there usually."

"But what're you doing here?"

"Taking care of Papa."

"But you, alone? You're my age, aren't you? How can you live here alone?"

"I'm thirteen," said Susan. "And I don't do it alone. Bethanne Morris comes in three times a week, to make suppers and clean up some. Papa goes up and down. Sometimes he's walking around, back and forth, looking out the windows, getting himself a snack. But other times he gets so old and nodding that he really needs to be carried around. I can't figure out any pattern to it myself."

"I'm twelve," said Daniel. "I never did anything like taking care of someone."

"Well, thirteen's old enough to 'know my own mind,' as Papa says. My parents think he's taking care of me. They don't see him being old and needful. So I put my foot down and said I'm staying here, and they don't care too much. A learning experience, they said. They'll be back up here in the summer as usual. But this is the first time they let me stay here all year."

Daniel was impressed. "Don't you miss them?"

"Of course I miss them," said Susan. "But I don't miss Miami. Sooner or later they'll be firm and make me come back. But they wanted to travel this winter. My father's business is hotel furnishings. They're taking a Grand Tour: hotels from Miami to Houston to Philadelphia to Miami again. They'll be back up here in June."

Susan splashed. Daniel watched. It got dark as they talked. "You can close those windows now, and I'll build a fire. Papa can't take the cold anymore. He sleeps on this couch, because it's too cold upstairs—and too many stairs, anyway. I'll make eggs and sausage, and he'll forget that his burned. He'll think he helped out by making dinner."

"I better go," said Daniel.

"Bring Papa from the other room, will you? My hands are full."

He didn't want to. But Susan was busy, arms full of logs and a poker and dangling kindling, legs kicking aside the screen at the fireplace. Her competency intimidated and challenged him. She wasn't any older than he was, after all, and here she was making supper, building fires, and taking care of her grandfather, as responsible as an adult. Daniel had never even made supper for himself.

So he crossed the hall to the other room, which was sunk in shadow. The thick backs of old upholstered chairs were clustered together like tombstones in a churchyard. One chair held Isaac Barrey. It rose over him like a shell, its wings protecting him from drafts, its arms sturdy at his side.

"Susannah?" His voice was dusty, like the air.

"No. I'm Daniel Rider—from across the lake."

"Hmmm." Mr. Barrey held up his arms.

Daniel stood there, the cold whistling at his ankles, his brow suddenly steamy.

"Well, come on," said Isaac Barrey. Even in the dark Daniel could see the purple of old veins showing in his face.

As if he did it every day of his life, Daniel leaned over the chair. Isaac circled Daniel's neck with his arms, and Daniel slid his hands under his knees and around his back. He lifted him, and a trailing plaid blanket, and carried him out of the dark room, across the hall, into the bright room, which still, despite its airing, hinted of smoke.

"Ah, Papa, dinner's all ready," said Susan, clattering china. "Daniel will stay for dinner, won't you, Daniel, for eggs and sausage? Put Papa there, in the big pine chair. There's plenty to eat, Daniel—stay."

"I can't. I'm late already." Daniel settled Papa in his chair. The old man was no bigger than a child, and his skin ran on his bones like the white over the yolk. He disregarded Daniel and picked up his fork.

"Well, thanks for stopping when you noticed the smoke," said Susan, tossing her dark hair back and suddenly looking her own age again, shy, still. "You can come back sometime, if you want."

"See you in school tomorrow," said Daniel. "Goodbye, Mr. Barrey."

"Mmphh," said Isaac Barrey eggily.

So the odd mist had been smoke from a scorching supper.

It was even colder now; the sun had yielded to the rushing black. Daniel abandoned caution and scraped his way across the ice of Canaan Lake, sliding and striking long trails in the surface. The thin, dry snow blew up in his face, and the stars came out, lonely and fragile and piercing. He was so vulnerable to the night, here in the center of this lake, unprotected by roofs or trees or passers-by, here in the center where the night was open and endless. A fierce wind, driving down the corridor between the mountains, could whirl him away like a leaf, swoop him off the planet, lodge him forever in the night sky, among the voiceless stars.

He was scaring himself. He ran toward his own home and thought about the lights around the lake, the golden squares of windows at his own house, and the Myer House, and Susan Barrey's house, and the houses in the village. And he reached his own golden squares quickly.

His mother was making gravy and his father doing the bills. "Oh, just in time," said Mrs. Rider. "Two minutes more and you'd have been out of luck."

When they'd sat down and said grace and passed around the food, Mr. Rider said, "Well, what happened today?" He was always at his most affable at the dinner table.

"I tried my hand at bread again," said Mrs. Rider. "It's a real challenge."

"Oh, do we have homemade bread? Where is it?" said Daniel.

"We don't exactly *have* it," said Mrs. Rider. "Discretion advises you to ask no more questions about it, and to tactfully change the subject."

"How goes the fight to make sense of the church ledgers?" said Mr. Rider.

"Slowly. Daniel, did you get that Ogleson contract I wanted?"

He'd forgotten all about it. "They couldn't find it."

"Oh, those . . . you wouldn't believe it, Bruce, their filing system is as arbitrary as the weather. I found a whole folder of canceled stamps someone was collecting—with the unopened envelopes still attached."

"You'll set them to rights. I hope you submit a good bill for your efforts."

"No, it's donated time," said Mrs. Rider. "And, you know, I rather enjoy getting things into working order."

"You should charge. You're worth it."

"I wouldn't trust a check from that account." Mrs. Rider laughed. "Oh, isn't that terrible. I shouldn't say that. No repeating that, Daniel."

"Who'd I repeat it to?" said Daniel.

"Oh, you must know some of the kids by now."

"These kids," said Daniel, "have been trained since birth to avoid any outsider. They do it all summer long when the vacation hordes arrive. I am classified as a summer kid stuck out of season, that's all. I'm perfectly qualified for ignoring."

"Oh, there must be someone," said Mrs. Rider, "some *one* kid who might be a possible playmate?"

"Mommy," said Daniel, "I'm twelve years old. I haven't

had a *playmate* since I went to the Lollipop Nursery when I was four. I have either *friends* or *enemies*. Mostly enemies."

"Some one person who might cross over?"

"Well," said Daniel, "I did talk to someone today. She's not a friend. But I talked to her."

"Good for you. Who is she?"

"Someone in my class at school. Susan Barrey. She lives across the lake, on North Road, next to Grobers'. She lives with her grandfather, who is old and burned the dinner. Her parents live in Florida."

"That's a funny setup," said Mrs. Rider.

"I remember Isaac Barrey," said Mr. Rider suddenly. "He had that house even when I was growing up here. He used to be the caretaker at the church, and did some carpentry on the side. His wife died soon after their son was born—Isaac Barrey, Junior, who was a bit older than I. Hmm. Susan must be Isaac Junior's daughter."

"Well, Isaac Senior is as old as the hills. I had to carry him to the table."

After some more eating, Mr. Rider said, "So you were by the Myer House today, too?"

"Yup."

"You'll wear out your welcome, Daniel. And don't say 'yup.' "

"They have a guy there named Nikos Griskas. He's a friend of Father August's. His sister dumped him there; he's sick or something."

"Well, then, you'd better not pester him till he's better."

"Did you ever hear of the Nesbitt thing?" Daniel said.

"Not me."

"Me either."

"Me either," said Daniel. "But I want to find out."

"Well, as I said, don't become a pain in the neck."

"Mommy *told* me to go."

"A profitable day," said Mr. Rider to his wife. "I got my own files in some sort of order, and an outline for the April thing, and several requests for commentaries. Jack Preston called again to see if I'd cover the convention for them."

"I'm delighted," said Mrs. Rider. "I knew your business would follow you. You're too good to let go."

"Well, one is never sure until it happens. But the office is beginning to shape up. By next week I should be on a regular schedule. Getting a new routine down takes some doing. Eh, Daniel? You're getting used to the new school routine, eh?"

"It stinks," said Daniel. "Your new routine is fun because it's all just you and all your old regular guys. All you've changed is your place of office. I have a whole new school of unfriendly hillbillies to deal with."

"Don't you dare," said Mrs. Rider, "hillbillies, indeed! You'd never have called your grandmother that, Daniel, and she was born and raised in the mountains. Don't be so snide."

"And I was born and raised here," said Mr. Rider.

"It takes time to get accustomed to things. Don't worry," said Mrs. Rider.

"You'll do fine. You're a born winner," said Mr. Rider calmly. "Pass the chicken, Marion. Delicious."

"Thank you. Daniel, did you get ashes yesterday? I forgot to ask you."

"Yes, I did." He parted his bangs, but there wasn't much left of the smoky smudge that Father Marston had thumbed onto his forehead yesterday afternoon after the disappointment of Father August's departure. Daniel had been in line, and the church had been noisy with the squeaking of rubber boots as parishioners filed up to Father Marston. Breath vaporized in the cold church. The candles issued ribbons of velvety smoke. The incense blended with the mothball smell of winter coats. Father Marston had been deliberate and soft-spoken, delivering the sign to his congregation that Lent had begun that day, Ash Wednesday, and that there were six weeks of feasting and penance and prayer to prepare for Easter. Daniel had lowered his eyes as Father Marston's thumb sought his brow, and Father Marston had spoken the words personally to him, Daniel Rider: "Remember that you are dust, and to dust you shall return."

"More vegetables, anyone?" said Mrs. Rider.

Chapter Three

Susan Barrey looked for Daniel the next day.

She sat with him in the cafeteria, though he knew he wasn't looking particularly friendly. They shared their lunches. She had carrot sticks and celery sticks and some thick bread. He had peanut butter and jelly. They bought some soda and Cheese Twists, and Daniel pretended to ignore the glances and jeers tossed at them by their classmates, who were amused at the unconventional arrangement. The rest of the boys, sitting together by the soda machines, and the girls together by the windows, observed Daniel and Susan's sitting together. Ed Gourney, the class commentator, made some remarks. But Daniel and Susan, both of them more or less new in the school, went on despite the commotion they were causing. And Daniel found that they had a lot to talk about.

"The Nesbitt thing," said Susan, idly dunking a carrot stick in her soda. "The name sounds familiar—but there are a lot of families who live in Canaan Lake and I don't know them. And there are summer people, too, tons of them. People who come to the mountains for the summer. Like my parents. Maybe Nesbitt is the name of one of them."

"If it is a local person, my grandmother would have known him or her," said Daniel. "But she died three months ago, at Thanksgiving. That's how we came here— my father inherited the house. He grew up here himself."

"Your grandmother probably knew my grandfather," said Susan, "because he's lived here his whole life, too. What was her name?"

"Carolyn Rider," said Daniel, and for a moment he missed her deeply.

"Well, we'll find out the story behind your friend Nikos," said Susan. "Can't you write to your priest friend?"

"Father August? Nope. Didn't leave me his address. He didn't even really say goodbye."

"What do you mean? Did he say goodbye or didn't he?"

"Oh, he *said* it," explained Daniel, "but it was so hurried. He didn't have time to *talk* to me. I thought somehow that there'd be more, that's all. I mean, he's my only friend here in Canaan Lake, even if he is older than I am."

"Sounds like a great friend," said Susan, crushing the ice between her teeth.

"It's the way he is," said Daniel. "He pays attention to religious things and stuff and forgets the normal, everyday routine. When he's looking at you he's *really* looking at you, and knowing you hard, but if you slip out of his field of vision, he looks just as hard at whatever else is there. It's the way he is: he's kind of brilliant and dumb at the same time."

"Even if you're brilliant or dumb, you can still treat

your friends right," said Susan. "You're defending him for being thoughtless."

"I guess I'm not saying it right, then. He's not thoughtless. He's overflowing with thought."

"Well, you're not everyday normal, so he ought to pay more attention to you."

"I'm not?" Daniel felt his scalp tingle. "I'm not?"

"For one thing, you're ridiculously loyal," said Susan, "if you're not furious at him for all that."

Daniel didn't have anything to say just then, so he folded the aluminum foil into an accordion shape and played it.

"Father Marston must have his address," said Susan when the concert was over and the foil was rapidly becoming a miniature shiny pyramid.

"I think August wants to be all alone—no letters, no messages, no noise. I couldn't write to him except in a life-or-death emergency."

"Well," said Susan, "leave it to me. Meet me at my locker at three. We'll go into town and see what we can find out." She crumpled her paper cup and shot it into the basket.

So when school got out and most of the students had climbed into the yellow buses, Daniel and Susan walked to town. The leafless trees were casting sad shadows in the weak February sunlight, and the square was quiet and deserted.

"The market," said Susan.

Jason Meister's market was the unofficial center of town. Essex County notices were always being tacked, one on top of another, to the weathered door. The people who didn't have phones, the ones who lived up in the hills, received and left messages taped to the silver sides of Jason's ornate old National Cash Register. And Jason Meister himself, large, booming, deaf in one ear, and newly launched into a second marriage with Vera Malecki, was the expansive soul of communication.

"Daniel Rider," Jason roared, his voice thick with a German accent. "I delivered the order to your parents' house yesterday. I forget something, what?"

Daniel stood over the grate in the floor, from which heat was streaming. Snow from his boots fell and melted. "No, nothing was missing that I know of. I just came because I was walking by. You know Susan Barrey?"

"Of course," said Jason. "And her father Isaac Junior and her grandfather Isaac Senior. How is he, Susan Barrey, well? The winter getting him down?"

"A bit," said Susan. "He seems to be able to get around by himself a lot better when it's warmer."

"I ought to stop by. Where does the time go," said Jason, unloading cans of peas from a carton and marking them with big black numerals. "I've known him for years, and used to help him out around the church. I remember his wife, too—a big woman come up here from Schenectady to marry him. Your grandmother was a large woman, Susan. When she died, it was a terrible thing. Of course, it used to happen often, deaths from childbirth. Still, Isaac Barrey was devastated. I used to visit him then—we'd sit on the dock and have nothing to say. He's a good twenty years older than I am, but after all that, marriage and a son and death, him involved and me a neighbor, we'd still have nothing to say. He's a quiet man.

"And you know, I really ought to stop and see him," said Jason. "It's been years since I've made a real visit, or had more than an exchange of hellos over the cash register. You get so busy, though, myself with the store and then my own wife dying, and my remarrying Vera Malecki. You get caught up in your own life. You know how it is. The time just marches on, as they used to say in the newsreels."

Susan said, "Mr. Meister, did you ever hear of the Nesbitt thing?" She held two potatoes as she talked, weighing them in her hands.

"The Nesbitt thing," said Jason Meister.

Susan selected two more potatoes, set the four of them on a scale, and looked at the grocer.

"That's two pounds of potatoes," and Jason marked the paper bag. "Out of five. You got six cents? Good. Change, here. You're wondering about young Nikos Griskas there in the Myer House, aren't you? Vera told me you hauled him in, Daniel, without the ecclesiastical okay. Poor chap."

Daniel said, "Tell us."

"You could've read it in the papers, had you a habit of reading the papers," said Jason. He leaned on his counter, picked up a Farmer's Almanac, and flipped its pages absentmindedly. "Nesbitt was a friend of Griskas's. From Washington, D.C., I think. They studied together at some college there. He was visiting Griskas, who's from Glens Falls, you know. They were backpacking in the mountains last month, and they got caught in that terrible below-zero weather we had at the end of January. And somehow or other, Griskas's friend Nesbitt froze to death. Griskas had gone for kindling or something, and got lost, and struggled all night, moving to keep alive. And Nesbitt, alone in the tent, fell asleep and somehow or other froze to death. Hypothermia, they call it, or something like that. They had to take his body down on a snowmobile. And it seems to me that Griskas feels terrifically guilty over this —though the state troopers said there was nothing to blame him for, except maybe getting lost. If Griskas had spent the night in the tent, he'd probably have died of exposure too—terrible unexpected Arctic cold."

Susan and Daniel were uncomfortable in their warm coats, standing over the rising steam.

"I'm home, Jason," said Vera Malecki Meister, stamping in the front door. "Oh, Daniel, hello. And who's this?"

"Susan Barrey," said Susan.

"Old Isaac's granddaughter," said Jason.

"How old was Nikos Griskas's friend?" asked Daniel.

"His own age," said Jason, dropping his voice. And Vera, flinging off her parka, her plastic beads rattling free, scolded. "No need to tell the little ones everything terrible in life, Jason! Really, I bet you talk to the frozen foods when no one else is here. Such a mouth."

Jason smiled and rolled his eyes.

"Now, Daniel, I want you to take this candy bar; you can split it with Susan. Go ahead, a gift."

"No, thanks. It's Lent. I don't eat candy during Lent."

"Oh. That's right. Well, some other time. Jason, there's a terrible drip from the faucet of the kitchen sink at the inn. Could you fix it tonight before you go to your barbershop singing, please? I'm going to start supper. Fried trout and onions. So long, kiddies." Vera clattered up the stairs to the second floor, and Jason got to his feet.

"So now you know about the Nesbitt thing," he said. "Don't go bothering poor Nick Griskas. He's got a hard time ahead of him. Sensitive sort—may never get over it. He's a poet or something. Writes books."

"So now we know about the Nesbitt thing," said Susan as she and Daniel left the market. It was almost dark, the night came so fast this time of year. "I'd better get home, Daniel, and start supper for Papa. See you tomorrow."

"Button up your coat," said Daniel.

Susan looked at him.

"Well, we should keep warm," said Daniel lamely.

He walked alone along Route 103, toward the home in which he and his parents were still so new. The light from the sun was fading fast. He came to a stretch of road that ran right along the lakeside, where a row of leaning, barren birches divided water and road. He stood next to a birch tree for a minute and watched the distant shore. He could see the lights across the lake, twinkling, jewels in the deep-blue shadows, the lights of the Grobers' and the

Barreys' and the house where the two Mrs. McDonalds
lived. On the tree next to him, one last curled leaf stirred
in the wind, one leaf left over from the autumn. As if it
had been waiting for an audience for its detaching dance,
its release from the tree, it waved and turned on its stem,
and then lifted from the tree in an eddy of wind and began
to sink, as Daniel watched.

The mist was stirring. The strange lights and thick-
nesses on the other side of the lake.

Who's burning dinner tonight? thought Daniel. Could
Susan's grandfather have tried again to cook a meal, and
is that the smoke from some charred chicken or something? No, it isn't smoke, and it wasn't smoke that he had
seen the last time, either; he knew that now. It was something else. Something untoward, mysterious, fascinating.
He watched, breathlessly.

A mist. A fog. Those words weren't right, Daniel knew:
fog is cloud settling, cloud sleeping on the floor of its
room; mist is moisture rising, in the act of becoming air.
There was no cloud here, and it was too cold for moisture
to rise. A new word was needed to define this. So Daniel
stared, his passion for understanding awoken.

It was like condensed light, he thought, although he
knew—or he was pretty sure—that light couldn't con-
dense. But that's what it resembled: a great patch of
accumulated light, long and low and as full as the wooded
ridge that rose up above it. Light so dense that, shining
through itself, it created shadow, dimension, the semblance
of form. It did not shine; it was not like a mile of sun dis-

played on the northwestern edge of Canaan Lake. It would have burned them all to kingdom come if it had been light that shone; Daniel knew that. It was light that, by its immutable concentration, provided its own cloak. And so it was not unlike a mist, slowly, slowly rolling on the lake edge, blocking out the view of the vulnerable houses crouched like small animals at the side of the lake, their docks like paws frozen in the ice.

In the mist—in the light that was cousin to mist—Daniel could see—or thought he could see—change and movement. The vapors were not one solid color, not the uncompromising wet gray of night fog, but more like the shifting, shimmering movement of air above an over-heated motor. He strained to see, he leaned forward. It was so hard to tell. The change was so minute, sometimes he thought it was his eyes tricking him, his mind imagining things. But in the vapors there seemed to be movement: a deepening, a lessening, an undulating, ever so slowly. It was nothing recognizable, just a random throbbing of light mist and dark fog.

But it would give birth to something. It would not remain like this forever.

And then it began to fade, finally, and Daniel watched the lights of the houses begin to show again. It faded, not in patches, but in degrees. It simply was less and less present, until eventually it was not there at all.

Daniel breathed out.

Instantly something caught his attention; he leaped back, wrenching his left leg away so fast that he fell on the shoulder of Route 103. Something that was still had moved. An echo was dying out across the ice; he must have yelled. It was only a leaf, fluttering to the side of a snowbank.

It was the same leaf he had watched fall from the birch tree a while ago. But it was only now falling. It had stopped falling; it had paused somehow, frozen in mid-air, and he had forgotten about it; and then it had fallen, finally, terribly.

The long time he had stood watching the lights on the lake had been no time at all.

Chapter Four

Until Christmas the Riders had lived in a fourth-floor walkup on the Upper East Side of Manhattan. Daniel had had his own room, a small area crowded with books, Scandinavian furniture especially designed to make sensible use of every possible inch of space, and the model airplanes his parents kept giving him, even though it was two years since he'd had the urge to put one together.

But with Grandma's death, Mr. Rider had bought his sister's share of Grandma's house, and then moving men had carted all their furniture and junk up the New York Thruway and the Northway, past Poughkeepsie, Albany, Lake George, to the house on Canaan Lake. Daniel's mother, recovering from a bronchial ailment, slowly began the task of sorting through the accumulated belongings of years. Mr. Rider was more involved in arranging the newest phase of his career as a freelance political columnist and analyst. Daniel and his mother poked through drawers and bookcases and closets, coming upon whole drifts and dusty deposits of personal treasures, and Mr. Rider, who might have understood or explained some of it, excused himself from helping.

"I don't know what to keep or what to toss," complained Mrs. Rider to Daniel on Saturday morning as they burrowed through the closet underneath the stairs. "She wasn't *my* mother. Really, he ought to be looking through this stuff." She pulled out an old plank with a dreary snowscape painted on it. Blue letters below read *Blizzard of '88*. She stood it on the telephone stand and said, "This is a hand-done thing. It must have some family significance."

"Just throw it out if you don't want it," said Mr. Rider, coming downstairs to deposit three manila envelopes with the rest of the outgoing mail.

"But whose is this? Was it your grandmother's? There's no signature, no initials," said Mrs. Rider. "And it's so quaint."

"Quaint is for antique collectors. I say just chuck it."

"But Bruce, for crying out loud, *look* at it. Someone in your family must have—"

"Whoever it was is dead and gone and I have no feeling for it. We don't need the place crowded with a lot of relics, this isn't a museum." He pounded back up the stairs, his footsteps thudding like hammer blows on the boards above their heads. Daniel thought, He's escaping to his room just as I would if there was something I wanted to avoid.

Mrs. Rider sighed and sat back, her nails black with the dust of years. "I'll make a list of these things and ask his sister Sharon about them. In conscience I just can't junk this stuff, which has been in the family all these years."

"Why not? He has," said Daniel. "He doesn't care what happens."

"Oh, he does, too," said Mrs. Rider. "I just run out of patience trying to pry it out of him."

"Well, I've helped for an hour and a half. Can't I go now?" said Daniel. "I mean, it's Saturday and all."

Mrs. Rider looked around her. "This stuff just swells. It looks worse than when we started. Sure, go on. I'll have a cup of coffee and try to be brutal when I get back to it."

Daniel grabbed his jacket and scarf and raced outside, throwing arms through sleeves only when he was out of sight of the house.

He had an appointment to keep. He walked fast, his heels digging splintering pockets in every stretch of ice along the road, his long, white scarf trailing like a flag. The cold had gotten in all the colors of the world: dimming pine green to olive, paling the blue of the sky, bleaching the noses and cheeks of boulders with ice. The cold was in his clothes, too, crinkling up the legs of his jeans, grabbing up his sleeves at his wrists and forearms. He shivered, and walked faster.

She was there, standing on the steps of the Canaan Lake post office, leaning on the stone lion. Daniel felt a leap of heart inside him and ran the last couple of yards, throwing his hands on the lion's neck. Susan said hello.

"It's too cold to just stand around. Let's get walking, and we'll talk on the way," said Daniel. "Button your coat."

"I'm not cold."

They strode off, out of the village, back the same way from which Daniel had come, toward the Myer House.

Daniel had thought of calling Susan last night, to tell her about his second experience with the lights. But he finally decided against this plan. He and Susan were still new to each other, not yet certain of friendship. To a friend, you could speak quickly between classes, saying, "The world is on fire," and you could expect to be believed absolutely, though there was no time for talk, since the next class was beginning. It was the strength of friendship that supported this trust; true friendship was a bridge between people, over which you could push anything you wanted to share.

But with someone new, you hesitated. How firm was the bridge, could it stand up under such astonishment? On Friday, Daniel had resisted calling Susan up. The phone was no good for discussing such things.

Now, as Daniel and Susan were walking along Route 103 two abreast, time was curling around them, and space, sweeping down the wooded ridges across the road, across the lake, and Daniel began to test the new bridge.

Susan listened, training her eyes on distance.

Daniel talked carefully.

He explained all about his first trip to Canaan Lake, at Thanksgiving, just before his grandmother had died, and the strange things that had happened then.

"Well, strange things do happen," said Susan.

Encouraged, Daniel told her about the lights. Not smoke from a burned supper, he said, it was something else. It was coming at him, at them, from across the lake.

And when it was there, shimmering and misty and mysterious—time was stopped.

"Time can't stop." This was her first objection.

"It did. It was. I thought I was standing there for an hour, mesmerized, staring. But later on I realized it had all happened—well, if in a second, it was the longest second in the world. No. It was like a crack in between seconds. If you can imagine that."

Susan jammed her fingers in her pockets.

"I know it sounds crazy," said Daniel, desperate.

But Susan said, "Oh, it does sound crazy, Daniel, but so what. Everything *sounds* crazy. But what is it, and why is it happening now, that's what we're going to have to find out."

Daniel's feet left the ground; he walked with energy. The bridge wasn't collapsing.

The Myer House came into view, around a stand of pines. Daniel felt something like a cold hand reach in around his heart and remove something, so his heart, in compensation, beat harder, making him shiver. He was missing August. And the missing had a real hurt, like cramps or spasms.

"What're all the cars here for?"

"I don't know. We can ask Mrs. Phalen or Father Marston."

Mrs. Phalen was hacking away at a side of beef with a great steel knife. A lock of hair was bouncing up and down on the side of her face, freed from the tight bun on her head. "A stew to serve twenty," she said, when Daniel and Susan went into the kitchen. "No trouble at all, Father Marston, I've nothing better to do on a Saturday afternoon; sure, the carpet in the chapel needs vacuuming and the plants are dying for a drink of holy water, but what's that to me, who sits around all day eating bonbons and reading trashy novels?"

"Whoops," said Daniel. "Bad timing."

"You haven't *heard* of bad timing, in your youth and grace, you child of God. Would you rub some salt, not too much, in this meat while I get to peeling potatoes, and maybe your friend would lend a hand?"

"Susan Barrey, this is Mrs. Phalen," said Daniel quickly.

Mrs. Phalen tried to jab the bouncing lock into the rest of her hair. "Oh, of the Isaac Barreys up a ways?"

"Yes," said Susan. "Where's the potato peeler?"

"If I remember correctly, it's stuck in the pot of philodendron, to have something to wind those sprawling tendrils around. On that side table. Plant will just have to sprawl. Wash the peeler off, and here's the potatoes in this bin. How's the old man?"

"Papa? He's fine. Shaky on his legs but looking forward to the spring."

"Aren't we all. Too much salt, Daniel, you'll choke us, might not be a bad idea. He's got fifteen gabbing ladies from Troy making a retreat this weekend, and he forgets to write it in the book. Sam's upstairs making beds. How Father Marston will quiet them down is beyond me. They come for a weekend of quiet meditation and they yak like a Geneva conference. The only thing that silences them is services—though they'll have enough to talk about, dirty carpet and dying plants. Oh, no one knows the cross I bear!" Martha Phalen grabbed a pair of kitchen scissors and clipped off the jouncing curl. Susan gasped. "If thine eye offendeth thee, pluck it out," said Mrs. Phalen cheerfully. "Time to serve tea to the Ladies Who Pray." She grabbed a potholder and an enormous aluminum kettle which had been steaming on the old stove, and whisked it out into the dining room.

Daniel rubbed salt. Susan peeled, and the spirals of peel dangled to her knees. She was good at it.

Mrs. Phalen came back and located a dozen onions and a paring knife. Onion tips wheeled crazily.

"How's Nikos?" said Daniel.

"Wasting away like the plants in chapel," said Mrs. Phalen. "I can't say why, except he doesn't eat much and he doesn't get up and he doesn't seem to hear what I say. No wonder I didn't recognize him at first. His face is sunken and yellowing. I remember him visiting Father August a couple of times; he was such a fine, strong young man, and happy, and expressive. Now he hardly seems to recognize me. I think Father Marston ought to get hold of Father August and have him come home, but then what do I know, being only the housekeeper and cook."

"We found out about Mark Nesbitt," said Daniel.

"Well, the world is a public place," said Mrs. Phalen. "I don't see any reason to go spreading the news. There's folks in Canaan Lake would be less than charitable to Nikos Griskas, feeling he might be somehow to blame for poor Mark Nesbitt's death. I met Mark, too. He and Nikos stopped by here and had dinner with Father August and Father Marston the night before they went camping."

The chattering of the ladies in the dining room had lessened as they sipped tea; Mrs. Phalen's voice dropped. Her knife cut off the onion ends and dry skins. Her eyelids shone wetly.

"They sat around the fireplace, smoking cigars that Mark had brought from Washington. They were talking about hiking and theology, and Nikos recited a couple of his poems by heart. Sam and I had gone in to sit by the fire, too, as we sometimes do. Father August took out his flute, and Nikos tried to play that old guitar with the warped neck, and Mark sang some songs. He wanted us all to join in, but his voice was so pure and high, a real Irish tenor, that none of us could bear to sing against it, we just wanted to listen. Then Father Marston broke out some ouzo—that's a Greek liqueur, you know; Father August being Greek, and Nikos too, it was appropriate. Then Sam and I went up to bed, but we could hear the four of them laughing and talking on into the night. And three nights later Mark Nesbitt was dead. Oh, he had a nice way about him, and now he's dead." Mrs. Phalen wiped her cheek with a sleeve. "Father August tried to get hold of Nikos, but he had disappeared. Once the police released him, he just vanished. Father August sent him letters; called his apartment down in Albany; called his sister in Glens Falls, that terrible Filoretti O'Toole I talked to on the phone; even called his publisher in New York City looking for him. But he was gone. And then, a month later, Father August goes off to the monastery in New Mexico, for six weeks of prayer, and Nikos shows up on the doorstep, dumped there by his sister."

Samuel Phalen came clomping into the kitchen. He nodded at Daniel and Susan, and put on a pair of old thick gloves and a red coat. "Going into town to plow out the church's parking lot, Martha; beds all made upstairs."

"He might be trouble, that Nikos, but I won't throw him out nor will I let them even talk of it," said Mrs. Phalen energetically.

"No one's talking of throwing the poor guy out," said Mr. Phalen patiently. "You need anything at Meister's?"

"Tell Jason that we'll have dinner with him and Vera next weekend; tomorrow'll be too busy, with this gaggle of geese in the house. Just that, and try to be home for dinner, Sam, please?"

"Gotcha." Her husband winked at them and left.

"Is there anything we can do for Nikos?" said Daniel. He had finished with the beef and sat on a stool near the deep sink.

"Lord knows he needs help," said Martha Phalen, "though the best I can give him is solid food and clean sheets. Father Marston's tried to talk with him, but Nikos doesn't seem to hear. If Father August were here . . ."

Oh, if Father August were here, thought Daniel.

"But enough gabbing. I'm as bad as those Troy ladies. If

I don't get this stew started, we'll all go hungry tonight."
She started quartering the potatoes Susan had peeled.
White potato juice beaded on the knife. "Don't suppose
you'd care to vacuum the chapel carpet, either of you?"

"No, thank you," said Daniel. "We came to see Nikos,
actually."

"Well, can't hurt, I don't think—" and Martha Phalen
paused, knife in the air. The interruption was caused by a
sudden silence from the dining room. And then Father
Marston's voice quietly said, "Sam. Are you in the kitchen,
Sam? Come here, please."

Mrs. Phalen leaped up and went through the swinging
door, Susan and Daniel at her elbows.

The ladies with teacups, sitting at the large table and
smaller tables, were all looking at one another or at the
floor or in their teacups. Father Marston had risen from
the head of the center table, a napkin still squeezed in his
hand. At the doorway stood Nikos Griskas, dressed in just
a towel around his waist. His eyes looked empty.

"Now, there, Nick, now, now." Father Marston crossed
the room quietly.

"Where's Mark?" said Nikos in a funny, desperate
voice.

"Now, then, Nick," said Father Marston, putting a hand
on his shoulder.

The ladies began to whisper among themselves.

"Sam's away at the church," said Mrs. Phalen, weaving
swiftly between the tables. "Now, Nikos, not here. Let's
go upstairs and I'll get you some clothes on your back."

"Mark?" said Nikos, and he looked at all the ladies.

Mrs. Phalen turned him around and guided him into the hall. Father Marston followed, and Daniel and Susan did too, closing the doors behind them. A great heated chattering bloomed in the dining room.

"Martha Phalen, we can't have this!" said Father Marston, helping her guide Nikos up the stairs. "The house will be full of ladies all weekend. Daniel, you've overstepped your place, I've been meaning to say that to you—"

"We'll talk about it later," said Mrs. Phalen through gritted teeth. "Kids, you'd better scram for a while."

Nikos suddenly said, "Mark!" and lunged to the window at the stair landing. He peered out, shivering.

"That's Bob Karner come to look at the pipes," said Mrs. Phalen quietly. "Come on now. Upstairs. That's it."

Nikos's head bowed, and his body relaxed between Mrs. Phalen and Father Marston. They each put an arm around him and carried him into the spare room. Daniel and Susan were left at the stair landing. The door to the spare room closed.

They were peeling potatoes, diligently, carefully; their attention to every eye and scrap of peel proved their concern. When Mrs. Phalen came back in the kitchen a half hour later, sighing, she didn't remark on their help. She began simmering the stew meat and handed them a bunch of carrots to slice.

The kitchen was equipped for preparing enormous

meals, since it was a function of the Myer House to welcome visitors who came to escape from the pressures of
their daily lives, to pray, to meditate. Mrs. Phalen often
had to feed twenty or twenty-five. The shelves and cabinets
were stocked with enormous kettles and pans; long utensils
hung like weapons from hooks; the pantry shelves held
dozens of plates. Mrs. Phalen looked shrunken, standing
among the oversize pots. Yet she managed, Daniel could
see, by moving like an athlete: twisting, reaching, bound-
ing from refrigerator to pantry to stove to table, sure in
her footing, determined. She had gotten the stew well
underway and was washing lettuce for a salad when she
realized that Susan and Daniel were still there.

"Oh, you're waiting. Of course. Father Marston and I
had a few words about Nikos. And the result of our dis-
cussion is that he's been moved out to the room over the
boathouse. Not to my liking, and I'll make that known
right now. But that's where he is. And if you are set on
seeing him, go on out. Maybe you'll do him some good.
Lord knows, I can't figure him out."

They left her chopping tomatoes, fierce as an execu-
tioner.

The boathouse was an elaborate two-story building, set
on a firm cropping of rock twenty yards out from shore.
When the estate had belonged to Aaron Myer, a lawyer,
a causeway had been built to connect the rocks with the
shore; a slate walk lined by poplars led out to the boathouse now. In the bottom the boats sat; there was also a
staircase to the second floor. They climbed it slowly, care-

fully; its steps were covered with ice. Daniel's knock went unanswered. He opened the door.

Nikos Griskas was sitting with his back to them, looking out over the lake. He was dressed in a thick sweater and jeans, and a fire was just beginning to rage in the woodstove that stood in the fireplace. The room was very cold. Nikos didn't seem to notice.

"Hello, Nikos," said Daniel. Susan stood behind him, close to the door.

"I came to see how you were," he said.

Nikos finally turned. Daniel felt again a blaze of confusion consuming Nikos. The young man's eyes were red-rimmed, his hands rattled uselessly on the edge of his chair. He looked as if he might wake up any minute from a strange daytime dream. But he didn't wake; his eyes didn't quite focus.

"I don't know what else to say," said Daniel finally. "How are you?"

Nikos opened his hands. He lifted them up; he wasn't quite shrugging, he was showing them that his hands were empty. His fingers slowly curled over the palms, over the emptiness. And then the hands dropped.

Susan said, "He doesn't want us here."

Daniel said, "He hardly knows we're here," and stepped forward. "We're sorry," he said. "Would you like to go out for a walk sometime?"

After a time, Nikos nodded.

And then they left.

"A long day," said Susan, "just to see him. Peeling potatoes and carrots and all that. And then only seeing him for that short time. But you're right, Daniel. There's something really wrong with him."

They were standing at the edge of the Lake Road, in front of the Myer House. Clouds were lowering, cloaking the crests of the nearby mountains, and the wind had stopped, so the cold air was piercing and still. Snow would fall before morning. Daniel stamped to keep warm.

"But there're lots of people who are sick," said Susan. "Why do you feel an obligation to him?"

"Why do you feel an obligation to your grandfather?"

"That's different. He's a relative. I've known him for ages."

"It's only different on the surface. Nikos is August's friend, and August isn't here. Besides, I'm the one who took him in." And we're both leftovers, thought Daniel. But he didn't say that.

"There isn't much we can do."

"I know." Daniel sighed. "But we have to try. For Nikos as well as for August."

But what?

All the way home, Daniel puzzled it out. Nikos was grieving for Mark, and his grief was made of loss and guilt. The loss and the guilt were like demons in Nikos; they had sprung up in the shock of Mark's death, and they had spread like plague through the roads of nerve and the fields of muscle and the rivers of blood, till the whole land of Nikos Griskas was ravaged. Grief had flooded his eyes so they didn't see; it had shaken the foundations of his thinking. Daniel could see that grief was not a fair fighter, and it had stolen Nikos; Nikos was an occupied territory, waiting to be liberated.

How do I know this? Daniel asked himself, arriving home and helping himself to a handful of Oreos and retreating to his room. His parents, immersed in various projects, hadn't noticed him come in. He sat on the edge of his bed and stared idly at his desk, tapping his fingers on his knees and sensing the forlorn night creeping up close to the windows. How do I know about Nikos Griskas, and about the army of grief holding him prisoner?

And Daniel's moving eyes settled on the browned photograph of his grandmother as a girl.

Chapter Five

Twice in the following week Daniel saw the lights on the lake, and he was certain that time was stilled or overcome or that it escaped when the lights rolled.

Susan Barrey was patient enough. "It's not likely I'll ever see them, since my house is on the other side of the lake from yours and you always see them from the same side."

"You should come over to my house some evening," said Daniel. "I want you to see them."

"Oh! What a line!" yelled Ed Gourney, who'd been listening from the next table. "Gonna take him up on it, Sultry Susie?"

Susan got up and stood at the end of the long table at which Ed Gourney and company sat. "A suggestion for you," said Susan. "Eat up and shut up." With a sudden movement she slid her tray roughly down the tabletop; food spilled and drink splashed all the way along.

"Hoo! A spitfire!" Ed Gourney mopped soda off his face with his tie. "Hot stuff, Rider."

Daniel and Susan left and walked upstairs to their lockers. "I shouldn't have done that," said Susan. "Now there'll be no end of trouble."

"I wish I'd thought of it," said Daniel.

"Oh, small matter. I'm just sorry we were interrupted. Is there any pattern to when you see the lights?"

"None that I can tell. It's happened morning, afternoon, evening. And I've seen it from my house and also the Myer House. I've always been right at the edge of the lake."

"Well, I'll come over—maybe tomorrow. It's Saturday, it's the first of March, maybe we'll be lucky. I'll give Papa some lunch and see you in the early afternoon."

Waiting for Susan, Daniel sat in his room and took out his journal. He was trying to write some poetry. The paperback volume of Nikos Griskas's work, *Nineteen Degrees East,* had been read over and over, and Daniel knew everything about it: the copyright date and the dedication page and the table of contents and all the poems, and the white pages at the beginning and end, and the comments reviewers had made that were emblazoned across the back cover ("Chilling. Incisive," said John Tremont). The picture of Nikos, in a white shirt open at the neck, sun spilling through his curly hair and down his shoulders, and a big white smile for the photographer or the reader (PHOTOGRAPH BY MARK NESBITT, Daniel noticed). Daniel's fingers even knew the slippery gloss of the paper cover, and the rougher paper inside. He knew where to contact the publisher for permission "to quote in whole or in part any portion contained herein."

He knew everything about the volume of poetry except what the poems meant. They sat on the page so legitimately, dense black type, a forest of lines and curls and dots all growing close in the great white space; Daniel felt sure they must be good poems, saturated with meaning, making people leap up in awareness. But he couldn't understand them.

He tried. There were lines, words, images that he nodded at, but the relationship of lines was difficult to understand, and Nikos Griskas seemed to forget to punctuate. Sometimes there were quotes in Greek and Latin at the top of the page; Daniel wondered if these were succinct foreign translations of the lengthier Griskas versions.

So he liked the contents page best, because he loved and understood the titles of the poems. "On the Passing On of Wisdom." "Athens, 1974." "An Orange in the Hand." "Sonnet to Figs and Treason." Figs and treason! Someday he would understand that poem; he could barely wait.

Meanwhile, he was trying to write some poetry, but it all sounded like Nikos's poetry, and Daniel couldn't even understand it himself. So he made lists of rhyming words. Sorrow borrow tomorrow. Lake shake take wake break. The only word that rhymed with Daniel was spaniel.

Susan arrived with a present. "It's from Papa. He remembered you," she said, pulling off her coat and looking around the room with interest. Daniel opened the cigar box. Inside was a piece of paper, a luminous lemon-yellow, folded and bent to look like a bright bird dipping to land.

Daniel held it up to the light. "It's wonderful. Did he make it himself?"

"He did, and it took all morning. It's origami paper; it's an Oriental art. He can do it sitting down, and he enjoys it. He has a couple of books on it."

"I'll get some string and hang it in my window. Hand me my scissors, will you? Top drawer." Daniel jumped on a chair and tied one end of the string over the curtain rod. "There. The first bird of spring, on the first day of March! Tell him thanks a lot."

"What's this?"

Daniel jumped off his chair and grabbed his notebook. "You can't see. It's private. It's my notebook. It's nothing about you or anything—it's just private."

"Oh." Susan put her hands in her jeans.

"Don't you have a notebook?" said Daniel, a little ashamed of his forcefulness.

"No," said Susan. "What for?"

"To write things in. To write down things." Daniel tried to explain and knew he was floundering. "So you don't forget."

"What things?"

"Facts. Stuff. Things that happen, things you think, what you see."

"Oh." Susan looked surprised. "I never thought of it."

"Well. It's private, that's all."

"That's okay," said Susan. "I don't mind."

"Yes, you do," said Daniel, "and so do I, but I can't help it. It's private."

He put it in the bottom desk drawer, and he put *Nineteen Degrees East* in on top, and stuffed a blue sweater on top of that. "This isn't to protect it from you," he insisted. "But in case my parents come in. I don't think they'd go looking for it, but they might see it by accident if I left it out."

"My parents would snoop if I had a diary," said Susan.

"It's not a diary. It's a *notebook*."

"Okay!"

Daniel's mother looked up as the two children clattered down the stairs. She was pale, with a red bandana looping her skull, and she was breathing heavily, leaning against the old piano with a pile of ancient newspaper clippings in her hands.

"Grandma had cut out every article about Canaan Lake to appear in any magazine for the past fifty years," said Mrs. Rider. "I can't bear to just toss it out."

"Toss it all out," said Mr. Rider, appearing from the dining room with an armload of logs for the fireplace. "We can use it for tinder."

"I'll save it for you, Daniel; you might find them useful doing a social-studies project someday." Mrs. Rider straightened. "We'll just never be through all this, Bruce."

"Why are you lingering over everything, Marion? Anyone would think you expected to find hidden treasure or lost deeds in all this. I'm perfectly open to the idea of hiring men to cart this stuff to the dump, you know, you needn't feel so responsible for it all."

Mrs. Rider sighed. "It's not hidden treasure, but it's important. It's like turtle shells and abandoned birds' nests. This stuff is the packing of your mother's life. It seems sinful to be so casual about it."

"Well, this fine-tooth-comb bit is up your alley, I know that. Just so you don't feel obliged. You don't want to tire yourself out. The doctors all tell you that. A little at a time, Marion. We're not in any rush."

"We'll be back later," said Daniel.

"Stay for supper, Susan," called Mrs. Rider as Daniel and Susan were leaving.

They trudged through the snow to the edge of the lake. The mountains looked nearer today than usual: the lower ridges seemed close enough to touch, each shivering limb of tree distinct, each bough of pine finely needled. And the higher peaks, Saltbook and the Two Sisters and Trapper Knob, seemed dense and immediate, not misty backdrop.

"The air is clear, in honor of March," said Daniel. "Look, you can even see Pine Slide from here, up on Turner Ridge."

"What's that?"

"A good place; I'll take you there someday."

"I've been up on mountains in winter before," said Susan calmly. "Two years ago we went skiing in Switzerland over the Christmas holidays."

"Oh," said Daniel.

"The Alps are so high, they're like walls. They're not like these mountains here, so old and worn down that you can almost see over them."

"Oh," said Daniel. "Well, I don't think these mountains are so small."

"It's just in comparison." Susan was mushing snow in a pattern, pushing it into several piles. She sat in the snowy hollow she'd kicked clear. She looked like a little general of an army, commanding from a throne, thought Daniel. Where does she get such confidence? From traveling to places like Switzerland, maybe. Daniel was unsteady suddenly in their new friendship: what would Susan want to be friends with him for? He felt his face go a little stiff, a decided model-boy look forming on his lips, his brow. I don't want to be stiff with Susan, he said fiercely to himself. He turned away, threw his glance out over the lake . . .

"Susan, look."

Daniel was pointing, gasping, his face open again.

"Oh, my God," said Susan.

The mist had arisen, shining; across the ice it stood, and there was that same random motion in it. Patches of gray light swirled around patches of brighter light. It seemed as if the areas of light were working to arrange themselves as something. Daniel kept imagining that he could recognize forms in the light, but just as he would be approaching recognition, and the word was descending onto his tongue to describe it, the forms would change, and in the alteration Daniel's recognition disappeared.

Susan was entranced, her hands up to her temples in dis-
belief, her dark hair thrown back, her coat unbuttoned,
her mouth open.

The radiance billowed and bowed, and the sun was forgotten.

"It's moving," said Daniel suddenly.

Up till now the snowy peak of the smaller Sister had
been visible above the mist. But the mist was expanding
upward; it remained on the ice along the far northern
shore of Canaan Lake, and its top lifted into the air. For
a while—although this is no while, this is not time, Daniel
thought, stunned—the mist had taken the form of the
smaller Sister, but then the mist spread upward again.

I can almost see its sides heaving light to the top!

The edges of the mist were clearly defined: there it was,
and then there was the regular sky behind it. But the edges
circled and spun, eddies of tireless light, and the mist was
building to a point, its sides sloping, its lake edge station-
ary. It was a mound; it was a mountain; and it was building, slowly, slowly seething. Some incomprehensible pro-
cess at work, Daniel thought, inevitable. Like the slow
explosion of a volcano. The lights were a mountain, a volcano, and then—a moment of equilibrium was estab-
lished.

The sides were equal: bottom and two slopes. It was a
perfect equilateral triangle pulsing shadowy light, its peak
twice as high as the mountains behind it.

"Oh, oh," said Susan, gripping Daniel's arm.

It wasn't through.

The peak of the triangle began to lift higher still, and it seemed to be pulling the strength from the light beneath it. There was a sudden shining of light, a dazzling, world-eclipsing instant.

And then the top of the triangle broke off and unfolded, out of its light, wings and feathers and a bird's head; it flapped once or twice, receiving the density of earthly objects and thus absorbing the cold light of a Saturday in March, and the bird flew toward them.

The mist was gone, and time was cranked up again and running on schedule. A truck roared by on Route 103. The bird came over the ice at a great height, but sinking as it neared the shore on which Daniel and Susan stood.

They fell to the ground, trembling.

It grew darker as it coasted, and but for its inception it would not have attracted attention. Its feathers were black as ink, and its wingspan a good two feet wide. It came so near, ten or twelve feet above their heads, that they could hear the wind in its wings. It circled, and then flew up toward the roof of Daniel's house.

"God in heaven save us," said Susan, scrabbling to her feet. "Get up, Daniel. Are we to follow that bird or destroy it, is it an angel or a raven, what are we supposed to do?"

"There's no telling," said Daniel.

There was no need, then, to wonder. The black bird

raised its head and opened its eyes. The light of the mist rolled in its eyes. Suspended above the house, pulling storms through Daniel and Susan, it cried in a loud voice.

A black feather fell like a leaf, making pendulum loops in the air. It fell right into the chimney. The black bird disappeared.

Chapter Six

"That's ours," said Daniel. "That feather is for us."

"How do you know?" said Susan.

"It came to my house. There's no other way of interpreting it. We'd better get it."

"Up on the roof? How can we even get up there?"

They surveyed the house. The long roof sloped down to the tops of the second-floor windows. Tall, thin evergreens crowded the house, but these trees were too spindly to support their weight. Outside the kitchen door leaned an old weathered trellis, with a browned rosebush and icicles entwined through the lattices: too flimsy.

"There's a skylight," said Susan. "Can we get into the attic and out on the roof through that?"

"It looks like the only possibility. Come on."

"Back so soon?" said Mrs. Rider. She looked like Buddha, sitting cross-legged on the floor, with yellowing documents and letters arranged around her in piles. Daniel told her that, and she laughed. "I wish I was that goddess with three sets of arms. It would make this sorting easier. Here's a whole sheaf of letters, Daniel, that your grandfather wrote to your grandmother before they were married. She kept them all these years, bound with a strip of lace. I haven't the heart to throw them out—and I haven't the nerve to read them. I just look at the dates and signatures.

The earliest one is 1930. 'Dear Miss Matthews,' it starts. And now they're both dead and buried west of town."

Daniel's father passed through with another armload of split logs. He dropped it with a crash in the living room and came back to stand in the doorway. "Don't be so sentimental."

"It's not sentimentality, it's respect," said Mrs. Rider mildly.

Mr. Rider looked quickly, and then turned away from the pages spread out on the floor. "I'm going to start a fire; it's freezing in here."

"Don't throw that stuff away," said Daniel to his mother, and then louder, "No, don't start a fire, Daddy!"

"Why not?" His father squatted on the hearth, constructing a pile of firewood and kindling.

The feather had fallen in the chimney, way up overhead, and who could tell if a fire might not damage it or burn it or make it explode? Daniel stood on his toes, staring wordlessly at his father, unable to invent a good excuse.

"Well," said his father, "going once, going twice—"

"He's too embarrassed to say it," said Susan suddenly, "but I'm allergic to wood smoke."

"Oh. That's a valid point," said Mr. Rider. "Health factors involved. You shouldn't be embarrassed to speak up about that, Daniel. I'll just put on a sweater instead."

Daniel and Susan went upstairs, and stood in the hall till they heard Mr. and Mrs. Rider begin talking about something else, and then they opened the door and climbed the attic steps.

It was a small attic, a dusty pyramid of space crowded with crates and invalided furniture. The chimney rose through the center of the attic room like a kiosk on a Paris street corner. Into the mortar, nails had been pounded, and oddments and remnants hung rakishly, as if on display: a curling calendar dated 1937, some framed photographs faded beyond recognition, a string of shells festooned on two nails, drawings, a pair of socks. It had been someone's special storage place. And there was no time to look more closely.

The wooden hatch was not far from the chimney. There were four rusty hooks holding it in place. It didn't swing out or in; instead, it lifted off, like a lid, and Daniel could see it needed to be brought inside very carefully or it would slide off the roof.

Even undoing the hooks was a problem. The wood was swollen and the hooks tight in their eyes. Susan and Daniel tugged and grunted and got rust swirling around in the dimness, but they didn't manage to release the hooks till Daniel went downstairs and took a hammer from the kitchen.

"They're going on and on about their childhoods now," said Daniel of his parents. "We're safe for a good long time, I bet."

A couple of blows from the hammer loosened the hooks, and the hatch began to lift. But then it stopped, and even though Susan and Daniel lent their shoulders to it, it was still stuck.

"Well, of course," said Daniel suddenly. "It's got a whole winter's worth of snow and ice weighing it down. This is like swimming underwater and coming up to find the top of the lake all frozen."

"So what do we do now?"

"Increase efforts," said Daniel, and he began again, getting a little start and ramming himself against it.

"You'll break your neck." But Susan did it, too.

Daniel made a sound like a locomotive, and railroaded into the square of wood; ice cracked, and a rod of light appeared. One edge was free, and working the other three free was easy. Snow trickled into the attic and wet the floor. When they finally managed to lift the cover up, and turn it and bring it through the opening, shards of ice and chunks of snow slid in with it, littering the cold, dusty attic with handfuls of winter.

But the sky beyond was blue. Daniel stuck his head up in the light. "It's less winter up here than down on the ground; the sun is nearer," he said. "You can even feel it a little." Susan pushed up beside him and found it was true. Beneath them, the woods and the frozen lake and the snowy yards and mushy driveways and the rises of rock were all ochers and umbers and steel-grays; all bound by ice and the temporary laws of the season. But above! The sky seemed to billow, cloudless, expanding; and the sun was making a go of it, testing its strength. It wouldn't win, not yet, of course, but it was exhilarating to know it was trying.

"I want to rid the roof of ice," said Daniel suddenly.

"I want to do my part." He ducked back in the attic and found an old broomstick, naked of bristles. He began to pound on the ice that overlapped the gutters.

"The feather," said Susan.

"I know," said Daniel. "But I want to do this, too."

"Well, then, let me help." Susan began breaking off fistfuls of snow and tossing them off the roof.

They became immersed in the project. The more they accomplished, the more driven they were to keep on. Stretches of slate roof, exposed to the sun for the first time in months, gleamed wetly and gave off a satisfying smell. When Daniel dislodged a key chunk of ice at the corner, and a whole protesting continent of snow rolled over the eaves, Susan laughed and clapped, and Daniel threw the broomstick, like a spear, up into the sky. It arched and wobbled, and then fell, gracelessly, near the toolshed.

"And now to the chimney."

They turned and looked. The roof rose like a great pyramid above them, crowned by the blood-red chimney. The old slates wouldn't afford much purchase; they were still wet. It wasn't far: eight, ten feet; but losing balance, and falling backward . . .

"Now what?" said Susan.

"Hmmm." Daniel stared. "Probably making a quick run is best."

"There's no way to get any momentum and no place to catch yourself if you start falling."

"But there's also no other choice."

"Let's see." They lifted themselves so they were sitting

on the edge of the opening, with their backs to the road and their eyes to the chimney rising over them.

"If you brace yourself on the edge and lean up the roof, and if I use your hands for footholds, maybe I can reach the chimney and pull myself up," said Daniel.

So Susan climbed out the hatch and fell against the cold roof, her arms stretched above her. Daniel took a deep breath and scrambled up the tiles, stepping on Susan's shoulder and then on her opened hands, and he was just able to grab the edge of the chimney and pull himself up to it.

"DANIEL RIDER!"

His father was a brown angry spike down in the white back yard. "What in God's name are you doing? Get down right now or I'll take a belt to you!"

"Trouble," said Daniel, standing up on the peak of the roof, hugging the bricks.

"Don't waste any time," breathed Susan.

"I can't find it. I can't feel it."

"We're in trouble. Will he be really mad? Come back in, Daniel."

"I can't find it. Where the—?"

The attic shook with the pounding of Mr. Rider's feet up the stairs.

"You'd better come back in before he gets here," said Susan. "We'll have to try again later."

"Oh, hell," said Daniel. "Oh—wait—"

Mr. Rider's head shot through the open hatch. Without a word he was out on the roof, stretched up next to Susan, his long arms reaching almost to the chimney. "Now let your-self down slowly into my hands," he said to Daniel. "Hold on to the chimney till I have your ankles. Don't go fast."

Daniel turned and sat on the peak of the roof. Suddenly he felt like a trapeze artist, the world arranged in rakish angles around him, his father's anxious face white as porcelain tilted up to him, his long, thin hands larger than the rest of him. Far away, down in the yard, a truck was pulling in the driveway.

He slid down, and his father caught his ankles, then his knees and his waist. When Daniel's feet were safely planted on the top ledge of the opening, Mr. Rider dropped into the attic and lifted Susan in, and then Daniel, as if they were puppies or babies.

The yelling rattled the whole house. Mrs. Rider, who was opening the door for the grocery delivery, left Jason Meister and a young helper standing puzzled on the porch. Mr. Rider's anger was loud.

"What's wrong, Bruce, what is it, tell me," said Mrs. Rider, rushing into the front hall.

"He's been out dancing on the roof, three floors above the ground, and a sure death if he happened to fall!" Mr. Rider's white face was clouding with red. Daniel and Susan stood accused and guilty in the middle of the front hall. Mr. Rider's incredulity blazed. And then the door from the kitchen crashed open and Jason came through. "Everything all right?" he said in his carnival barker's boom.

"Only just barely, evidently. Now, Bruce, don't get excited. Nobody's been hurt." Mrs. Rider put her hand on her husband's arm.

Jason looked at Daniel critically. "Been up to monkey tricks? Shouldn't worry your folks like that."

"What you were *doing* out on the roof is what I'd like to know," said Mr. Rider.

Jason's helper came in through the kitchen then, lured by the shouting. Just as Daniel opened his mouth to speak, he saw Ed Gourney standing at the edge of things, grinning.

"Ulph," Daniel said, and closed his mouth.

"Who's that?" said Daniel's father.

"My new helper. Lugs the cartons; I'm getting too old for that," said Jason. "You want to pay me now, Mrs. Rider, or drop it by next week?"

"Bruce, would you write out a check, please." Daniel's mother seemed dazed by all this.

"Hi, Daniel; hi, Susan," said Ed Gourney, a mockery of friendship in his voice.

"Daniel can't talk to you now, he's out of favor," said Mr. Rider from the living room. "Marion, where in blazes is the checkbook?"

"I think tonight's not a good night for you to stay for supper," said Mrs. Rider quietly to Susan. "Perhaps you'd better go home now."

"I'm partly to blame, Mrs. Rider, it was my idea," said Susan. "Please, I'm really sorry."

"Well, as long as no one's hurt. What happened, anyway?" asked Jason, sitting down on the stairs, capping his knees with his hands.

"Yeah, what happened, Danny?" asked Ed.

"NONE OF YOUR BUSINESS," said Daniel. "Come on, Susan, I'll walk you a ways."

"You'll walk to your room and no place else." Mr. Rider came in, flapping the check to dry the ink. "Here, Jason, credit us with any surplus."

Susan said, "Mr. Rider, I want to apologize—"

"Apologies won't mend a broken bone, little girl."

"Her name is Susan," said Daniel, starting to be disgusted.

"I *am* sorry." Susan flushed. "For whatever that's worth."

"I'm not going to put up with this type of behavior," answered Mr. Rider.

"All right already, leave her alone," said Daniel loudly, surprising himself. "Yell at me, not her."

"Don't you start," said Mr. Rider. "You're on shaky ground, son."

When Mr. Rider called Daniel "son," it was time to quake. His father used it not as a term of endearment but as a means of expressing regretful possession. It made Daniel sick.

"Daniel, you'd better go to your room, and we'll talk to you a little later," said Mrs. Rider. "Now, Susan, I think you'd be wise to go along."

"Fuss and turmoil at every stop today." Jason pulled himself to his feet and started jangling his key ring. "Kids cutting up here, and the Taylor's cat, Muckrose, got hit by a Mobil truck, and there's fireworks and hullabaloo at the Myer House over the young Greek guy—"

"What?"said Daniel, stopping midway up the stairs.

"No time for chatter," said Mr. Rider.

"Created a fright last night, he did." Jason's stentorian echoes rolled right over Mr. Rider's protests. "Woke up in the middle of the night screaming bloody murder. They heard him all the way to the main house, where there was a group of nuns on retreat. Four o'clock in the morning Father Marston and Sam Phalen and Martha Phalen go charging out into the snow in their nightshirts and floppy slippers—what a sight! With a convent's worth of nuns at their heels."

"So what was the matter?" said Mrs. Rider.

"Nothing but a bad dream. Can you beat that? Sam Phalen thinks they should call the county sheriff and have this guy taken away. And Martha Phalen, tough as nails— she isn't speaking to Sam this morning. And Father Marston's just as puzzled as could be. A bad dream. He was yelling loud enough, Sam told me, to wake the dead."

"Well." Mrs. Rider straightened her shoulders. "I feel sorry for the poor man. But maybe Sam Phalen's right. What good can come of him wailing away in the night?"

"Daniel, *upstairs*," said Mr. Rider in galvanized tones.

"Goodbye, Susan," said Daniel, but Susan had turned away.

"Want a ride? We're going your way," Jason was roaring at Susan.

Chapter Seven

Daniel closed his bedroom door and stood in the middle of the room. He took a deep breath. Then he unbuttoned his left sleeve and took out the feather.

He drew up his desk chair and put the dark feather on it; then he sat down on the edge of his bed and looked at the thing with objective eyes.

He said to himself, If I had found this by the side of the road, would I have known it to be fantastic?

It was nine inches long, tiny black threads growing out of a central white stem. The surface was smooth, as feathers are; the individual hairs still glossily intact, not dried and separated. It weighed a featherweight. It looked like any feather he might have picked up by the side of the road and carried home.

But it was different.

How is it different? said Daniel to himself. Figure it out!

It smelled like a feather (almost no smell at all). It was neither warmer nor cooler than a feather should be. It did not leave indelible marks on the seat of the chair. It did not even taste extraordinary (though Daniel had never tasted a feather before).

And yet it was different. Born of mystery, it retained

some mystery, some quality that Daniel felt he was too dull to isolate or comprehend, but was not too dull to perceive. It lay on the chair with the same qualities that any other feather had, yet it was different, and its difference was such that the house around him seemed diminished, drained of importance, pale by comparison. The feather on the chair somehow made Daniel feel he was being acted upon by a strength he did not know about.

His father's voice was cannoning up the stairs for him. Daniel ran to the top of the stairs and shouted down, "What?"

"I haven't got time to attend to you now: I have to take your mother into Elizabethtown to get her medication. I don't want you to go out of the house till we return, do you hear?"

"Yes, Daddy."

"We'll discuss your transgressions later."

"Yes, Daddy."

Daniel could see his father standing at the foot of the steps, trying to figure out what to say next. He was drumming his fingers on the newel post. "It's not so much your disobedience as the fact that you could have killed yourself that we're upset about," he called.

"Yes, Daddy," said Daniel, and he knew his father was being truthful. He also knew he was annoying his father with his monotone answers.

"So stay in."

As soon as the car pulled out of the driveway, Daniel grabbed his coat and his scarf and the feather and rushed out onto the frozen lake.

He wished he were running to see August. Maybe August in his quiet thoughtfulness would be able to look at the feather, understand where it had come from, know what to do with it. But in the absence of August, Nikos was the only other possibility. Maybe he would know. He was a poet. Didn't poets concentrate on amazing things?

As he ran and slid across the lake, ever further from the shore, into the vast exposed icefield open to the winds and the light, the face and form of August Petrakis throbbed steadily in Daniel's mind. What would you do? Why aren't you here, he said over and over, as if the repeated question might draw him back somehow.

The Myer House boathouse wasn't too far, by ice, from Daniel's house, and as he ran, sweating and panting, it grew larger and Daniel began to see the dark shape of Nikos Griskas sitting at a window. Daniel waved, but Nikos didn't respond. Daniel began to feel silly; he took off his scarf and circled it over his head, like a lasso, and he hooted for Nikos. But still there was no wave, no sign of recognition, though Daniel could see that his eyes were open and his head turned toward him.

Off balance from his crazy scarf-signaling, Daniel slid on his left heel and crashed down hard on the ice. He was not far from the boathouse, just six feet, and he cursed himself for falling when he was so near the shore. His hip and his elbow were numb, with the numbness that precedes a lasting pain, but he was more concerned with the feather, which he had put in his left pocket. In the aftermath of the spill he had inadvertently rolled on his left side, and what if the feather was torn or bent?

Even before he could roll onto his back, shifting his weight off the feather, there was a shock of cold all along his left leg and his waist and his elbow. For a terrible second he thought he was being gripped by paralysis; it was ripping through his left side, deadening the nerves, stilling the blood. Even his voice stopped its moaning, in the crash of this realization.

The world tilted, the boathouse threw itself forward, and just as Daniel suddenly knew that it was not paralysis but the water of Canaan Lake lapping at him, he was waist-deep; he was in water and the blackness of it was like all black nights condensed and descended at once.

When the blackness let its grip go slack, hands and lights were working at Daniel, pushing the cold back in him, insisting the warmth. The surface was malleable; in his deepness Daniel was a piece of stone being carved, altered, created, shaped. Voices began to ring like bells around him, distinct in tone but undecipherable in meaning.

One bell rang through to him, though, it was a sound he had not often heard: it was the voice of Nikos Griskas, striking above him somewhere.

A groan arose out of his imprisonment, and with it a

spume of nausea, which was wiped away. Daniel opened his eyes.

He was on his back on some towels in the chapel of the Myer House, and Mr. and Mrs. Phalen and Nikos Griskas were massaging him; he was stripped down to his underpants, which he knew would embarrass him tremendously when he stopped feeling so ill.

"So he opens his eyes," said Martha Phalen. She leaned back on her feet for a minute. "Can you speak, Daniel?"

"Romphrumph," said Daniel, and got sick again.

"He's as right as rain. Foolish boy. Easy to tell he's a newcomer to the mountains in winter. I'll go call Dr. Fell and have him stop around here on his way home tonight." Martha Phalen charged off.

Daniel tried to protest.

"Relax. Relax. It's all right," said the unfamiliar voice of Nikos. Daniel looked around for him. Nikos was leaning against the altar, his eyes wide, his stare steady. Behind him Daniel saw the crucifix gleaming gold, the Christ on it stylized almost beyond recognition. The sun was burning on a portion of the Christ's brow and the light was as welcome as those hands had been, dispelling the cold of the waters.

"You're conscious," said Sam Phalen. "Good. You went crashing through the weak ice at the edge of the lake, do you know that? After a warm day like today, you shouldn't go stomping on the edges of the lake. Though I have to admit I'm surprised. It's unusually early for melting ice. You carry a blowtorch with you or something?"

Father Marston came into the chapel, dropping his gloves and car keys, hurrying across the carpeted floor. "Martha called me from the acolyte meeting; what happened, Sam?"

"It's young Rider. Went through the ice near the boathouse. Our friend Nikos pulled him out and carried him here—the closest warm place. Martha's calling Dr. Fell now, but the boy seems okay."

"Well, get some clothes or a blanket for him, Sam; he'll catch his death of cold if he hasn't already."

My death of cold, thought Daniel, and he shivered, and threw up some more, and he wondered, as Sam was wiping his mouth, if he would be fighting the fingers of cold for the whole long rest of his life. If, really, death was nothing more than the extinguishing of warmth.

It scared him. Like a baby, he began to cry. Father Marston said, "There, there," and Sam Phalen left to make up a bed for Daniel. Nikos moved closer, on his knees, and held Daniel's hand. And the hand and his own tears were both warm, and that was some comfort, so he slept.

"We're becoming a regular hospital," said Father Marston, opening the door for Mr. and Mrs. Rider. "There he is."

Daniel came up out of his dream. His parents were sitting on folding chairs near his bed. Mrs. Rider had her hand on Mr. Rider's elbow. They both looked odd.

Father Marston sat on the edge of Daniel's bed. "So how are you feeling now, sport, after your bath?"

"Okay," said Daniel. His mouth tasted terrible. "Can I have a glass of water?"

"I'll get it," said Mr. Rider, and he left.

"Are you all right?" asked his mother. "How do you feel?"

"I feel the same way I did the time the subway broke down and we were stuck on it for an hour, only opposite. I feel cold."

"You don't seem warm." Mrs. Rider's palm felt good on Daniel's brow. "Mrs. Phalen says that Dr. Fell ought to be here in an hour or so. She thinks you ought to spend the night here."

"I'm sorry, Mommy," said Daniel.

"Perhaps I'll go prepare Tuesday's class on penance," said Father Marston suddenly. "Daniel's always welcome here, Mrs. Rider." He moved out of the room, nodding, bumping into Daniel's father in the doorway.

"Water." Mr. Rider handed Daniel a glass.

"I'm sorry about all this, about everything about today," said Daniel, after he'd gulped. "None of it was on purpose; I didn't want any of it to happen this way."

"I think you have a few explanations to go into, when you're feeling better," said Daniel's father. "You're not usually so disobedient."

"There's not much to say except I'm sorry," said Daniel, "and I'm glad I didn't freeze to death."

"Or drown," said Mrs. Rider.

"Or break your neck on the roof," said Mr. Rider.

"It's been a day of narrow escapes," said Mrs. Rider.

Every day is, thought Daniel; and then he smiled at the narrow escape from his parents' anger that he had just experienced.

Dr. Fell came in later. He thumped Daniel's chest and took his temperature and looked in his ears with a flashlight and in his mouth with a stick. "Any pains? Aches?" he said, while slapping his instruments back in his bag. Daniel didn't answer.

"Spend the night here, and be wrapped up well when you go home tomorrow. You want to be careful of exposure for a couple of days or you'll get pneumonia. Call me if there's a problem."

"Thank you, Dr. Fell," said Mr. Rider.

"I want him to come home tonight," said Mrs. Rider when Dr. Fell had trudged off. "I don't want him to stay here."

"You heard the man," said Mr. Rider. "We should make certain it's okay for Daniel to stay here. I'll check with Father Marston."

"It's fine," said Martha Phalen, coming in with another blanket. "I'll look in on Daniel during the night. If you want to take him home tomorrow after church, that'd be convenient for everyone."

"Well," said Mrs. Rider. She gripped her purse and smiled uncertainly. "I can't help but feel as if I'm abandoning you, Daniel."

Nonsense, said Mr. Rider and Martha Phalen, by bustling around and helping her on with her coat. "Goodbye, then," said Mrs. Rider. Mr. Rider gave Daniel a bristly kiss, Mrs. Rider gave him a perfumed one. Daniel closed his eyes as their faces came near his, the complication of their being both angry and relieved making their kisses quick.

"And by tomorrow," Mrs. Phalen was saying to his parents as they went filing out, "I'll have washed and dried all his clothes so that he'll be warm going home."

Not more intrigue, not more disobedience, thought Daniel, sitting up suddenly in the bed. Not another escapade in this long, involved day. But there was a chore to do: the feather. It was in his coat pocket. It couldn't be washed and dried. What would happen to a machine-washed, tumble-dried feather off a bird born of strange mists? He would have to get it.

But he was almost naked, and there was no robe, no towel with which he could wrap himself while he stole downstairs to the laundry. Lord, such involvement. He would have to use the rough brown blanket. And the Myer House was full of nuns. Well, with any luck, they would all be in chapel.

Night had come during Daniel's sleep, and the Myer House was warm and smelled of coffee. He felt like a very small child again, in a Superman cape, venturing out into the upstairs hall.

They had brought him to the third floor, where there were tiny cells and long dormitories for the visitors and guests of the retreat center. Daniel's white feet picked up dust from the floorboards. There were no nuns on the top floor.

But on the second floor water was running and a radio thrumming and voices twisting in conversation in other rooms. The long hall was empty. Daniel ran to the top of the stairs, leaned over the rail, and, seeing no one, dashed down.

At the door to the dining room he stopped; dangerous voices threatened. He retreated into a shadow. Father Marston was just emerging from the kitchen.

"You're being muleheaded about this," said Father Marston over his shoulder. "You know we have to think about the welfare of the whole house."

"And the welfare of the whole house is no better and no worse than the welfare of its individual members," yelled Martha Phalen through the door.

"He's not a member of this house; there are other places for him," said Father Marston.

Me? thought Daniel. Other places for me? I'm not wanted here? A cyclone suctioned his stomach and he thought he might spray the protective shadows with a sudden thunderstorm of tears and vomit. The excitement of being an overnight guest at the Myer House disappeared, and he wanted to go home, where they wouldn't kick him out. His nose dribbled saltily over his upper lip.

Martha Phalen kicked the door open and came in with a trayful of cutlery. She clinked forks down around the table, setting for tomorrow's breakfast. Every clink was a period to some statement. "He's a friend of Father August's. He's sick, yes, but his sister won't have him. So he woke us all up last night hollering like a banshee, big deal. He's sick, Reverend Doctor Mathias Marston. And who's to say he's not getting along somehow? Didn't he scrabble over the ice and pull Daniel Rider right out of the water?"

They're not talking about me, thought Daniel—it's Nikos. But that was cold comfort, the thought of Nikos being argued over and dispensed with, like leftovers; Daniel's internal cyclone maintained its fury.

"How can you say there's no room for him here? Where is mercy, where is compassion, where—"

"Martha, don't throw those words around," said Father Marston, disturbed. "Mercy takes many forms, and compassion as well; if Nikos Griskas is screaming in the night from some undissolved pain, perhaps he ought to be somewhere else, where the pain might be less."

"He isn't leaving," said Martha Phalen.

"It's not as if we're doing him any good," said Father Marston. "Just because Daniel Rider took liberties with our welcome mat doesn't mean that this is the best place for him."

"Daniel acted out of an instinct of kindness which I for one don't mind imitating. Nikos Griskas is not leaving." Mrs. Phalen leaned on the spoons. "I won't speak a word to you or Sam if you turn him out."

"A minor miracle," said Father Marston under his breath.

"Don't—" Mrs. Phalen's voice got loud.

"I'm waiting," said Father Marston quickly. "I'll give him a few more days to show some sign of improvement.

It's been two weeks, Martha, but for you I'll wait and see, a couple of days more."

"Not for me, you silly priest." Martha Phalen's voice suddenly became softer, grateful. "For him. For his well-being."

"All right, for him, then."

"Now the sisters are in chapel waiting for you. You're late. Go and be inspirational." There was an undercurrent of respect and grudging gratitude in her voice. Father Marston left, and Daniel held his breath as the priest hurried past him.

Away, then the slow tides of antiphonal chanting began, filtering in from the chapel through the living room. The muted, round voices of women at prayer, and the thread of Father Marston's special deep ecclesiastical voice, and the droning radio from upstairs; these sounds rolled on past Daniel in his rough blanket, into the dining room. Mrs. Phalen set out piles of cups and saucers on the sideboard, and then made an odyssey around the table, skirting the chairs and darting at the spaces to leave napkins on the left, water glasses on the right. She was working with precision, and her movement was a chant, too.

When the table was ready for breakfast, she stood for a minute looking at it. Daniel watched unabashedly. Mrs. Phalen looked sad for once, her rubbery hands resting on a chair's back, her head tilted uncharacteristically awry. "Sixteen for breakfast," she said, almost to herself.

Sam Phalen came through the swinging door. "Ahead of

yourself, aren't you," he said, pulling his gloves off and chafing his hands on her shoulders.

"Always," said Martha, and laughed at herself.

"So what's new? Supper go okay?"

"Supper done and dishes done and Daniel Rider's fine; he's staying the night in the little room over Father August's room, Dr. Fell told him to, and Nikos isn't leaving yet, at least for a couple of days. That's what's new."

"He's a problem, that Nikos," said Sam. "I think he should go get professional help."

"Oh, you." Martha Phalen shivered violently. "Well, he's not. He's here. And that's that. Now I'm going to go take a good bath."

"I'll be looking at the news," said Sam, heading for the parlor.

"Turn on the water in the washer in fifteen minutes, will you," Martha called. "By then I'll have finished running my bath."

"Right."

The laundry was a small cold room off the kitchen. Wicker baskets were stacked unceremoniously between the big square appliances. Sheets hung on lines, bisecting the room whitely, and a sting of small snowflakes was beginning to touch the cold black squares of window. The smell of starch mingled with the sweetness of dried herbs, which dangled, bunched and forgotten, on last summer's strings.

Daniel leaned and knelt, and moved about the room, the itchy blanket hot on his shoulders and back, the cold sucking around his bare legs and susceptible knees. There were piles of laundry like snowdrifts leaning everywhere, and he hated to disturb the piles, but the feather was crucial somehow.

Then he remembered, and grinned at his thickheadedness, and lifted the lid to the washer.

His coat and his jeans and his flannel shirt were all stirred together already, like chocolate and white in a marble cake, but he found a coat sleeve and yanked.

The feather was there; he dropped the coat back in the machine and let the lid fall with a clang. He turned and hurried like a secret agent, through the laundry, through the kitchen, into the dining room.

Nuns were conversing on the stairs, in the hall; remarking on the snow, on the schedule, on the loveliness of the Adirondack mountains, on the relief at being away from their usual routines. Father Marston was being sociable, although Daniel could hear in his voice a deepseated desire to be looking at the news instead. Finally, the stairway was clear and Daniel made a break for it.

"What the dickens—?"

Sam Phalen, at the door to the living room, scratched his head and grinned, and then went to turn the washer on.

Back in the room where he had woken up, back under the eaves at the northern edge of the Myer House, Daniel burrowed under the covers, teeth chattering, skin crawling with the cold. When he was warm, he sat up and looked at the feather, which had caused him a day of trouble. The rooftop, and the running over the ice to show Nikos, and the expedition to the laundry—

When will I show this to Nikos? Daniel thought, and he twirled the feather between his thumb and forefinger, staring at it—and a realization surfaced, between his fingers, as it were: the feather, the dark normal mystery feather, plunged into icy water six hours earlier, retained no moisture, no gluiness, no hint of its traumatic dunking. It was as dry and intact and smooth and unruffled as if it had been kept in a cigar box.

And that, marveled Daniel, is the proof I was looking for, of the feather's oddness in this world.

Chapter Eight

———————

Daniel awoke refreshed, energized. His clothes were folded on a chair next to his bed. He got up and dressed quickly in the cold air, and clattered down the stairs to the dining room.

"Feeling better, Daniel?" Father Marston waved a fork. "Take a seat. Sisters of various orders, meet Daniel Rider. Daniel, Sisters."

"Hello," said Daniel, sliding into an empty place. Sam handed around a platter of eggs, and the morning conversation ebbed with the smell of toast and tea in the warm room. Martha felt Daniel's forehead and poured him some orange juice.

"Service is in an hour," said Father Marston, suddenly rising. "Excuse me, folks. Better get going or I'll be late." The Sunday-morning services were held in the main church building in the town of Canaan Lake, a mile away; everyone began gulping last mouthfuls of tea and piling plates.

"No, you take your time, you didn't have any supper last night," said Martha Phalen. "I want you to eat all of that up. Your parents will be here by eleven-fifteen, probably, so you can do what you like till then."

"Doesn't Nikos have breakfast?" said Daniel.

"When I bring him something. Don't worry about him."

"I'll carry it over if you want."

"Well, you shouldn't be out in the cold. Doc Fell said so."

"I'm fit as a fiddle. I'll run."

Mrs. Phalen carried a full tray into the kitchen. "Well, eat up and I'll see. It would help me get to church on time."

Nikos Griskas was just waking up when Daniel opened the door into the room over the boathouse. "Breakfast," said Daniel, setting the tray down on a table. "It's probably all cold already."

Nikos sat up on the sofa and rubbed his eyes. "Oh," he said, and sighed.

"Eggs, coffee, toast, some little burned broken pieces of bacon," said Daniel helpfully, unwrapping the dish towel that Mrs. Phalen had folded over the food to keep it warm.

"Mmmph," said Nikos. With an effort, he drew the tray toward him and looked at it for a minute, dully, as if it were a sample of gravel and sand. He picked up a chunk of scrambled egg with his fingers, almost put it in his mouth, set it down again.

"What's the *matter* with it?" Daniel felt the slightest tinge of irritation.

"The matter," echoed Nikos. He looked at Daniel for the first time, and for a minute was pretending, or was trying, to smile. It certainly wasn't a very convincing smile, but the effort was a start.

Nikos drew the blankets around him, though he was fully dressed. He took a sip of coffee. Success! Daniel applauded silently. Nikos found a cigarette that had fallen in between the sofa cushions and lit it. The smoke swirled in handsome curves, resembling the stylized writing that Daniel remembered scribbled on trains in the New York subway. Nikos sipped and puffed.

"Where is the key to the whole thing, the catalyst, the translator," asked Nikos, "the ruler, the measuring stick between our comprehension of the world and the world itself?"

"Umm," said Daniel nervously. Nikos was talking like his poetry: riddles.

"The hint, the clue." Nikos listed, discarded words, looking for the accurate one. "The key, the emissary, the unbound?"

"More coffee?" offered Daniel, after a silence.

Nikos laughed. Laughed! and held out his cup. "In the absence of the key, coffee is a worthy substitute," he said.

Nikos took a sip. "I had a dream last night. I was in a large shadowy room, with high dusty plaster ceilings, and moldings and volutes and beveling." Nikos's eyes seemed to shrink as he spoke of his dream. "The dust ran in strings, festoons, between the towering tops of old furniture. I went to a sideboard to look for something, but in the carved wood of the drawers there were no handles. I couldn't open the drawers. And I went to a tall chest of drawers, and again the handles were missing. The room was crowded with dressers and desks and drawers and doors; I shoved furniture aside to find more furniture, and everything was stripped of its handles. The beveled doors to closets, the ornate double doors that led out of the room, had smooth, unknobbed surfaces. Nothing to grasp."

Daniel could understand this, at least, and he listened fervently.

"Finally, in a shadowy corner behind a wardrobe, I found a narrow door with a small brass knob and a key in the lock. I lunged at the door, to turn the key and twist the knob—and I had no hands." Nikos shivered. "No hands at the end of my arms."

"Oh, no." Daniel leaped up, appalled. "What a terrible dream." He shook himself, like a dog after a swim, to release the dream's impression.

"Mmm," said Nikos. He twisted his fingers in front of his face, realizing them. "I'm never sure whether to prefer the dreams or the days."

"But the days aren't terrible like that dream," said Daniel. He sat down suddenly on the bench of the old pump organ, left there from the time this room had served as a chapel. "Are they?"

Nikos smiled then, a real smile, and said, "You went crashing through the ice yesterday."

"And you pulled me out," said Daniel. "Thanks."

"Any time at all," said Nikos with a flourish. "How did you happen to fall?"

"I was waving at you," said Daniel.

"Oh." Nikos looked puzzled. "I didn't see you."

"You saw me fall through the ice; you must have seen me."

"I only noticed that by chance."

"How could you not see me? You were staring right in my direction."

"I was thinking of something else, I guess."

Daniel said, "Well, the ice seemed thick. I never thought it would break. It sure was a surprise."

"You weighed a ton, logged with water," said Nikos. "I thought you would die of the shock."

Suddenly Nikos seemed to be showered inside himself with a powerful rain. He sat up; the blanket fell from his shoulders; the cigarette sifted unbreathed smoke through his words.

"Why were you waving at me? Why were you coming?"

Daniel reached in his coat pocket.

He brought out the feather.

Nikos neither leaped forward nor pulled away; he didn't exclaim or gasp or lose his newfound clarity; but he looked at the feather and his concentration doubled, tripled. Daniel felt the energy: like the pulsing, ravenous flames of a house on fire. He remembered that he'd felt this from Nikos before.

"Where?" said Nikos.

"Out of a cloud," said Daniel. "I was running to show this to you because you're a poet. I thought you might understand what it is."

"It is—" said Nikos. "It is—"

Daniel's arm was getting tired, holding the feather up.

"But the whole world is too," said Nikos suddenly, heavyweight despair bearing down on him. "It is all a reminder, all imbued with the fuse: that time rolls on like a monster, eating everything up, swallowing everything up with its bleeding mouth, and we get swallowed up too. No saving ourselves from the mouth of the monster. The whole world is crackling with that *memento mori*." He paled. "Even a feather, even a bird's feather comes shimmering with beauty deserving of salvation, and of salvation there is none. It all comes down to dying."

He looked away, looked down, lit a cigarette, was lost to Daniel.

Time rolls on like a monster, eating everything up . . . It all comes down to dying. Oh, it wasn't hard to figure out why Nikos felt like this, when his friend Mark Nesbitt had died, had been swallowed up by the monster mouth; but Daniel wanted to show Nikos that there were other things too, things worth surviving for.

Daniel, sitting between his parents in the car on the way home, closed his eyes and thought about last Thanksgiving, when he'd first come to stay at Canaan Lake with his grandmother. The lightning had struck, and magic—

if that was the word for it—had happened: dangers and dancing and impossible things come true. He hadn't believed it at first, but he'd been shown by Grandma. When she'd died and the Rider family moved into her old home, the world had seemed poor and dark and mean. The mouth of time had swallowed her.

And there was no way of getting her back, no way in the world. Or Mark Nesbitt, or anyone dead. It didn't matter how much you missed them. They were all eaten up.

But there were other things in the world: there were other people and places and things; there was even this magic, breaking through the seams of the real world. It was the magic that Daniel had thought could shake Nikos out of his sorrow. But he seemed even more deeply entranced in it. There's Nikos, rejected by his sister, lost and floundering in his loneliness, Daniel thought, and here am I, Grandma and August removed from me. He's in a prison, and I'm in a prison too: caught in a room of loneliness, with no way to open the door. But I *want* to get out. If I can.

"You're a quiet one. You feel all right?" said Mr. Rider.

"Yes." Daniel was glad that his parents, however mystifying, weren't dead. "Dad, what's *memento mori?*"

"*Memento mori,*" said Mr. Rider. "Reminder of death. Something that makes you remember that you're going to die someday."

"Why ever are you asking about that?" Daniel's mother sounded worried. "And where did you hear of it?"

"Oh, around," said Daniel, enjoying the tiny consternations and the heat from the car on his knees.

"It's like the ashes you get on Ash Wednesday; that's a *memento mori*," said Mr. Rider.

"Why would you want to remember about death? I'd rather forget it if I could. I usually do," said Daniel.

"So that you remember about how important, and how short, life is, and so that you be good and live a good life."

"How short is life?"

"Sometimes it's very short," said Mr. Rider.

"But you needn't worry," said Mrs. Rider quickly. "You have plenty of time to grow up, and when you're older, it is a little easier to understand."

"Nikos is older and he doesn't understand it."

Mr. and Mrs. Rider exchanged glances; Daniel could feel them thinking to each other: We'd better stop letting him visit that Nikos Griskas. So Daniel said brightly, "But I don't care, it doesn't bother me and I never think about it. What are we having for dinner? Because I, for one, am starved."

But Daniel did think about it, *memento mori*, and it did bother him.

Maybe it was because of Daniel's accident on the ice, and his puzzling over death, that his parents didn't slam a punishment down on him, for all the disobeying he'd done. They had a nice supper, the three of them, all chewing determinedly at Mrs. Rider's sorry bread, and after dinner they were sitting at the fireplace when the doorbell rang.

It was Susan. So that his parents might not have the chance to say anything too parent-like to Susan, who'd been partly responsible for the roof-climbing incident yesterday, Daniel led her up to his room. "But what about Papa?" he asked, as they climbed the stairs.

"He's had his dinner and was very sleepy tonight. I put him to bed early. Daniel, I heard in church today that you'd fallen through the ice, so I had to come and find out what happened." Susan shed her coat and flopped down on the braided rug that Daniel had begged to keep in the room, along with the other old-fashioned furniture. The smart Scandinavian pieces were stored in the attic.

"I got it, I got it, I tried to tell you but couldn't get your eye." Daniel pulled at his blue sweater and his notebook and some Asterix comics, and underneath was the feather, in the bottom of the drawer.

Susan touched it with a reverent finger. "Now what do you suppose we do with it?"

"I don't know that, but I know this: even when I fell through the ice and was wet to my skin, the feather in my coat pocket stayed perfect and dry."

Susan leaned on an elbow. "But how did you fall through the ice, Daniel? The winter arrived late, but still it's been very cold. Papa says he's rarely known the ice to crack so early."

"I fell on it and it cracked."

Susan looked doubtful.

"I did," said Daniel. "I fell on my left hip, I still have a bruise the shape of Alaska."

"Where was the feather?" said Susan.

"In my pocket."

"Your left pocket."

"As a matter of fact, yes. How did you know?"

"An experiment," said Susan.

She threw open Daniel's bedroom window; a fluff of snow like dust sprinkled in from the sill. A row of icicles had been forming all winter from the rain gutter just above the top of Daniel's window. The icicles hung all in a row like frozen rags and bones.

"You'll freeze me out of here," complained Daniel. Susan grabbed the black feather and leaned out the window into the mountain wind. She ran the feather along the eave, at the high roots of the ice. And like wind chimes, like strung mollusks, the icicles clinked and clipped together for a few seconds, an eerie music, and then the whole curtain of ice sticks fell, thudding in the deep snow below.

"You melted the ice on the lake yourself!" said Susan, banging the window shut and holding the feather in her fist, upraised like the torch that the Statue of Liberty carries. "When you fell on your left pocket, the feather melted the ice. It has a heat all its own that you can't even feel with your skin—but it melts ice. It melts ice!"

Her face vivid with enthusiasm, Susan was a sight to see.

Something was beating on some surface, and the clues were all aural and none visual. It was the sound, the repetition—soft *thwup thwup thwup, thwup*—that suggested a beating. It was like the sound of soft large marshmallows plashing in a pond. It was like the sound of wet airy snow-balls thwupping on a window.

The snowball sound faded, but the image of the window lingered, a space of glass, a field of resistance. The sound changed. Now it was like someone's boneless hands slap-ping against the window. The arms were gone; just the boneless hands like loose sacks of snow and sand hit the window, forcelessly but tirelessly.

The black of his dream and the black of his bedroom at night collided. Daniel awoke in a cold sweat, his own hands tucked for warmth between his knees; he wasn't sure if he had screamed himself awake or . . .

The thwupping continued on his bedroom window.

He stiffened in his cold sheets, his voice useless, his mind capsizing.

Then he thought: It's Susan, throwing snowballs at my window in the middle of the night to wake me up; maybe the lights on the lake are back.

And he was brave, because if he'd been timid he'd have died of fright just then. He leaped out of bed, flapping in the funny nightshirt he'd found in one of the closets, and ran across the icy floor to the window.

The night was earthquaking at his window; it was un-dulating, disturbed, the way a landscape is shivered by the streaks of rain on a window. Daniel rubbed his eyes. Things fell into focus. The sight suddenly matched the sound. It was the bird, the dark fearful bird with the light in its eyes, hovering, beating its wings on the dark glass.

Again, fear would have killed him; thus he dared not be afraid. Daniel flipped the lock and lifted the window open.

The bird landed on the windowsill, hopped to Daniel's desk, folded its wings, and looked at Daniel.

"Oh, well, then," said Daniel, at a loss.

The bird seemed content with that. It closed its eyes.

Daniel brought it some water in the soap dish. He brought it the crust of his mother's terrible bread. He closed the bedroom window so that neither of them would catch cold. He laid the bird's feather down next to it. He spoke to the bird, asked it questions about the lights on the lake, about Nikos, about the bird itself. The bird showed no signs of answering in any way. In fact, it seemed to be asleep.

"Well, good night, then, and thanks for almost scaring me to death," said Daniel, out of ideas. "And I'll take my feather back *if* you please." He put the feather under his pillow and climbed back into bed. He didn't know why the bird was here, but something would happen sooner or later. He might as well sleep.

Soon Daniel was dipping into the richness of sleep thick like jelly; he was submerged in the slowing brilliance of dream, and the bird was with him, on his shoulder now.

The bird stretched its wings and began to fly. Daniel grabbed the feather from under his pillow and held it up in one hand, again like a torch or a flag, and he flew after the bird.

Off the bed through the window glass into the ebony night.

The night coiled outward from the earth, and in the cold clear air that pierced like gasoline in his nostrils, Daniel flew. Beneath them staggered masses of mountains and ridges and foothills and orchards and open fields and the kneeling shoreline and then the flat frozen lake. Above: stars cruel and small and foreign, some of them, but Orion blazed familiar and friendly; and there was a half moon the color of fresh cream.

The bird seemed to know its way. It kept at a steady pace, a constant height, tracing the sweep of the shoreline. Daniel followed, and the effort was minimal. He needed only to keep his elbows in; it was really the feather in his left hand that was flying. Perhaps I would fall if I let go of the feather, he thought. But I won't let go, I won't fall.

The snowy roofs of the village of Canaan Lake were dazzling in the moonlight. From the church's steep roof the wooden cross cast its shadow on the village green. They were descending now, spiraling around the cross, so close Daniel could see the paint flaking and blistering.

But they circled lower, wheeling past the Canaan Lake post office, where the stone lion stood covered with frost, past the boarding house, skirting the front of Meister's Market—and then flying at a window and through it.

Daniel scarcely had time to be frightened. From one level into another into another, he managed to think, even as he was aware that the bird had come to a pause in mid-air above the great snoring bulk of Jason Meister.

Daniel sank, feet first, not to the floor, but into Jason's dream. The dream took Daniel's ankles like a warm bath; it rose generously to his knees, his waist. Vera, Jason's wife of several months, did not seem to be dreaming tonight. Jason's dream flooded over Daniel's head.

I'll never get back to my real bedroom, he thought.

Jason's dream was bright and loud. There were too many things going on, like a carnival; Daniel was confused at first with the variety.

But somehow the bird was here, even in Jason's dream; Daniel knew this, though he could not see the bird. The bird led him through the noise and clatter to a silent corner, and the dream adjusted itself slowly, coming to birth.

A woman was at the cash register. She wore a red babushka over her long, oat-colored hair. Her nose was fine and big and her lips broad. In fact, she was big all over: healthy hips and breasts and strong arms and legs. She wore a black skirt and a white shirt and a pink sweater with buttons like pink cat eyes. Jason had given her that sweater one Christmas.

Her name was Alma. Alma Meister. She was attending the cashbox in the store. Her big fingers sorted the bills, which crackled like October leaves. Five ten fifteen twenty . . . there was a smile on her face. She did not look dead, but both Daniel and Jason, in Jason's dream, knew that she was. Thirty-five forty forty-one -two -three . . .

Alma Meister at a picnic table, spooning out mounds of potato salad onto paper plates. Everyone else in the dream was insubstantial and dimmed by Alma's luminousness. Her lips were red like the pimentos in the salad. You eat, more in the bucket, much more in the truck, she said. Her voice was red, too. Jason puts the potatoes in my kitchen and I make them into salad.

Alma Meister, younger, on a train platform. She was saying goodbye to Jason, she was going away to visit her sister, who was having a baby. She was thin, in black because her sister's husband had died in the war. She was trying not to cry. A porter ran the wheel of a luggage cart right over a pie she had baked for her sister. Jason was trying to fix the crust with his fingers, to keep her from crying. Alma kissed Jason. The kiss was not particularly short.

All aboard! came a voice. Alma Meister picked up her pie and a gray suitcase tied with rope. Take care of yourself, Jason, and don't forget to let the cat out before you go to sleep, she cried from a compartment, her hand out the window, the train pulling away.

Alma Meister at the çash register again, counting out the day's income. Five ten fifteen twenty . . .

At a funeral, in black and lace. The lace on her head had escaped its pins and was trailing all on one side. On a street, a street in Philadelphia, smiling for a camera, a bunch of lilacs in her arms. Plucking chickens in the back room, making soup, serving it with crackers to dozens of shadowy appreciative guests. The images whirled faster and faster.

But she's dead, Daniel and Jason remembered. She died last year of a collapsed artery.

As if to argue, she appeared again at the register, making change for a customer, counting it out: fifteen, twenty-five, one dollar . . .

Vera came into the dream, knocking snow off her boots. So you're married to Jason, said Alma.

And happily, said Vera, without malice.

I'm glad, said Alma. He always was fond of you.

And he's still fond of you, said Vera. They sat down together at a table to drink some coffee. After a sip Vera left.

I miss you, said Jason through his dream.

I know you do, said Alma, sitting on a dock and dangling her feet in the water.

I dream about you all the time, said Jason.

No one ever said it would be easy, said Alma. The setting sun lit her hair green and copper. She shook her head and caught a fish.

And you're gone, said Jason, growing desperate.

Ah, but I'm here in your dreams.

Come back to me.

I've never left you.

The dream began to go quicker, and its edges to blur. Alma was standing on the railway platform, smoothing her skirt, setting a pie down behind her so she could have both hands free to say goodbye to Jason. Her face had the clarity of real light in it.

And the dream drained out of the room. Jason was snoring. Vera was curled up close to him and their hands were clasped. The bird flapped its wings and flew out the window, and Daniel, confused and sorry for Jason, followed.

They made the return trip quickly. Daniel saw a pickup truck like a Matchbox toy, rolling along Route 103. It is real night, not dream night, he decided.

But through the glass of his bedroom window they passed, into the gentle, kind grays of his bedroom shadows. And when Daniel had alighted on the cold floor and set the feather down on his desk, the black bird hopped to the windowsill and tapped its beak on the glass.

"Good night, goodbye." Daniel opened the window, the bird flew away, and the boy crawled exhausted back into his bed and slept.

Chapter Nine

It was halfway through breakfast the next morning when Daniel remembered the flight to Jason's dream. He clanked his spoon in his cereal bowl. His parents both looked out from their sections of newspaper. "Don't clank, Daniel," said his mother. "Do you want some more oatmeal?"

"No."

"Light's changing a bit; I can feel it already. Can you, Marion? Sun's coming up earlier. Won't be long before spring."

"Well, brrr, I wish it'd hurry." Mrs. Rider hugged herself in her houserobe. "Next winter we've got to insulate this house better. I'm surprised your mother didn't freeze to death in all those years she lived here alone."

"Oh, she was a tough old bird," said Mr. Rider, discarding the newspaper and sipping coffee. "The place still seems funny without her."

"Did you know Jason Meister when you lived here as a boy?" said Daniel.

"Sure did. He's fifteen or twenty years older than I am, though; we weren't exactly friends."

"Did you know his first wife?"

"Alma Lantzig. Didn't know her well. She and Jason always donated the hot dogs and hamburgers for the St. Mark's June festival. A good woman, as I recall. But it's been years since I saw her, and of course she died early last summer. And Jason married Vera Malecki! I still can't get over that."

"Now, Bruce, Vera is a remarkable woman, as far as I can see," said Daniel's mother. "Capable, energetic, devoted to him—"

"Don't misunderstand me; I think it's great. Just something of a surprise. And for Vera, too, imagine that: adjusting to married life at age sixty."

"What happened to Alma when she died?" said Daniel.

"She was waked, probably right in Jason's house; funeral services at St. Mark's, I bet, though I think she was Catholic, not Episcopalian; and she's probably buried right there in the cemetery on the edge of town."

"But, I mean, what happened to *her?*"

"She's in the coffin, Daniel, in the ground. You know about that."

Daniel didn't know how to say what he wanted to say, so he clanked his spoon again in the bowl. A flower of milk splashed up.

"*Don't clank,*" said Mrs. Rider.

"Where did she go, Jason's wife? Where is she now?"

"Marion," said Mr. Rider, "you're the theology buff around here."

"Her soul left her body," said Mrs. Rider slowly, "and went back to God. Went to heaven."

"Oh. Well. So it's somewhere, at least; at least it isn't *nowhere*."

"As you wish," said Mr. Rider in a mild voice.

"Bruce!" Mrs. Rider clanked *her* spoon.

"Well, it's not a law can be proved, eh?"

"Can I have some more oatmeal now?" Daniel held up his bowl. "And can I bring an apple for lunch?'

"Only a little more oatmeal or you'll miss the bus," said Mrs. Rider. "And I'd rather not have to drive you to school today. I'm going to write to Sarah, and try a new bread-making technique. I'll get it yet."

"Doesn't matter if I miss the bus," said Daniel, slurping oatmeal, "I can fly to school."

"Oh ho, you'd better fly, look at the time," said his mother. "Quick, now. See you at three-thirty."

"I might walk home so I can stop and see Nikos," said Daniel, running out of the room and shouting over his parents' protests, "so if I'm a little late, don't go sending the National Guard out after me. See you later, bye!"

It was lunchtime before Daniel had a chance to tell Susan about the bird and the dream.

"I don't understand," said Susan, ignoring the commentary that Ed Gourney, two tables away, was delivering about Daniel and Susan's hot romance. "Did you dream you flew to Jason's store, or did you really do it?"

"I did it," said Daniel. "I think."

"And what a funny dream for Jason to have. How can that be connected with the feather, and the bird, and the lights on the lake?"

"Yaa, yaa, yaa," sang Ed. "What color should we paint the kitchen, Danny darling, yellow or blue?"

Daniel said wearily, "Let's go outside, Susan, where we can hear each other."

"Papa's not feeling well today," said Susan, when they were standing on the front steps of the school. "I don't think I should come to the Myer House with you. It's bad enough that I have to leave him alone all during the day."

"I'll call you if anything happens."

When Daniel let himself into the Myer House, he could hear Vera Malecki Meister and Martha Phalen chatting in the kitchen. Water was boiling and there was a sweetness in the air.

"Fresh bread. Warm yet, use butter, delicious," said Mrs. Phalen when Daniel appeared at the kitchen door. "Don't wait to be served, Daniel, or you'll starve."

Vera was finishing a crust. "I really should be getting dinner on, myself. I hired that Gibbons girl to do the cooking at the boardinghouse, but I forgot that cooking for two takes some preparation, too. Of course, Jason would eat anything."

"You wouldn't serve just anything, you're too conscientious." Mrs. Phalen diced celery as she talked.

"Well, this is a kind of retirement for me, being responsible just for the finances of the boardinghouse and not the actual overseeing of every chore," said Vera. "Lord knows, I've earned a rest. And speaking of resting, Martha, what's the news on Nikos Griskas? Jason came home the other day with a story that Father Marston wanted to send him along."

"Father Marston and my own Sam, both of them. But they've agreed to wait a bit."

"And Nikos?"

"Ah, Vera." Mrs. Phalen cupped her palms around the mound of celery bits. "If it's not one extreme, it's the other. If it's not the noise, the nightmares, the wandering around the house looking for Mark, it's something else. Quiet, no reaction to my words, scarcely a bite of food touched. I think he's dying inside. I don't know what else to think.

"Maybe," Martha Phalen continued, shaking her head, "maybe Sam and Father Marston are right. Maybe this place isn't the best place for him. Maybe a hospital . . ."

Vera got up and put her hands on Martha's shoulders. "Now just you wait a bit, Martha Phalen; spring is right around the corner, and we all feel better in the spring."

"Besides," said Daniel shyly, "Father August will be back in a month."

"Well, yes, there's that," said Mrs. Phalen. "I forgot for a minute."

Daniel's visit to Nikos might have been no visit at all. Nikos was stretched out on the sofa, with no blanket over him, though the room was cold and the fire dead. He didn't hear or see Daniel.

Daniel left the boathouse, misery settling in him. Was it that monster mouth of time that was eating Nikos?

The old rusted pickup swerved into the driveway. Mr. Phalen hollered, "I could use a hand hauling in this lumber, if you've time," and he parked between the kitchen and the shed. Daniel came up to the truck.

Sam drew on his tough, fake-leather gloves and sloshed through the parking-space snow to the open end of the truck. "Forgot that I promised Father August I'd get that bookcase up in his room," he said, "and the time's running fast. You want to help me drag this upstairs?"

"Sure," said Daniel.

"It's a weight, no joke," said Sam. "Picked it up at the Two Sisters' lumberyard. They let me select it myself, so I know it's good. Got your end?"

"Umpph."

The wood smelled good, like beginnings of things. Then Daniel got a sliver in his thumb. "Watch the newel post, easy," coached Sam as they struggled up the stairs.

They knocked over a stack of books someone had left on a table in the hall. "Ah, those are Nikos's things," said Sam. "I guess I should bring them over to the boathouse. You want to run over with them?"

"No," said Daniel.

"Don't blame you. Come on, let's get the next load. He's a real character and he's in for a bad time. I don't like the feel of what's coming. He ought to be getting professional help—"

They reached the truck again.

"The last time I saw Nikos before that awful death was right here in this house," said Sam. "Being a good friend of Father August's, Nikos had stopped here with Mark Nesbitt for the night. We all had dinner together, I even remember it was ham and cheesy potatoes. We toasted Nikos on the acceptance of his second book for publication. We toasted Nikos and Mark both, for success and luck on their hiking trip. I think Father August quoted something, something nobody understood, of course, and looking back, it was sort of Thanksgiving-like, because everyone was in such high spirits. Whoops, watch the wall, Daniel, or I'll be having to repaint the whole corridor."

"Did you ever know Mark?" asked Daniel.

"No. Of course, Nikos isn't from around here either, but he'd come to visit Father August several times, so we all knew him from that. But Mark Nesbitt wasn't a regular here. Oh, he was a pleasant guy, Daniel—well, like Nikos used to be. We were sitting around the fireplace, and he sang and sang. Had a nice voice . . ."

They stacked the last of the lumber on the pile. Out the windows Daniel saw the sky thickening with darkness. "I'd better go or I'll miss my dinner," he said.

"Thanks for the help," Sam said. "See you around."

On the way home, Daniel saw the lights again.

The mists weren't rising to a point, congealing and converging to become a bird or anything else. Instead—could this be possible?—they were illuminating themselves, pulsing toward definition, throbbing at form. The shifting patches of mist seemed to be shifting more slowly, more definitely . . . Oh, how Daniel stared!

Look carefully, he said to himself, so that when you give the report to Susan, you give it accurately.

He decided, eventually, that if he were pressed in a court of law to describe how the lights differed this time from the other times, he would say that the gradations of light and shadow at times seemed to be forming stripes, vertical stripes that wavered and pulsed, but were beginning to keep their shape. Is this some great pattern of stripes, breaking through into the world? A vast field of unearthly pillars coming to birth over Canaan Lake? He was sure now that the lights were more than just lights and mist. They were something else.

Stripes, pillars, lights, mist . . .

When it was gone, and time again went clicking down its track, Daniel walked home. Stripes, pillars, lights, mist.

A bird born out of mist.

Why did the bird take him to Jason's dream about his first wife?

Mist, stripes, lights, pillars . . .

Just what was coming?

"Hamburgers tonight, and your father's famous frozen french fries," said Daniel's mother when he got home. "Now you'll be sure to do your homework before you watch any television, won't you?"

"Where're you going?"

"Tonight's choir night," said Mrs. Rider. She looked nervous and excited. "I auditioned last week for Alice Garvey. She directs. We're going to be working on a Good Friday service. Look, she gave me all the music, so I could practice."

"You can't sing."

"Don't be so sure of yourself, mister. What do you think I've been crooning to myself all week long? The alto part to the Handel chorus we're doing on Good Friday. Just because I didn't sing in New York doesn't mean I don't know how." She straightened up from the mixing bowl, shreds of ground beef in her fingers, and sang in a watery little voice, "And with His stripes we are healed."

"Are you supposed to trill all up and down like that?"

"Yes. Now, remember, homework first, got it?"

"Got it got it got it."

Mr. Rider came into the kitchen. "Ah, time for a really great meal. Daniel, let's have supper in the living room and watch the news."

"Nothing doing," said Mrs. Rider. She put her coat on and grabbed her keys.

"While the cat's away, the mice will play," said Mr. Rider.

"This is one cat who's not coming back from choir practice just to vacuum the crumbs in the living room. Now, where's that bread I baked for Martha Phalen?"

"There in the pantry," said Mr. Rider, lighting the oven.

"Goodbye, you two, eat well, and, Daniel, your home-work—"

"I know, I know," shouted Daniel.

"Now, don't be late, honey," said Mr. Rider, kissing his wife.

"Oh, I don't know," said Mrs. Rider. "This might be a particularly high-spirited choir, given to celebrating after every rehearsal. Bye-bye."

Daniel followed his father into the living room with a plate of french fries and a hamburger and three under-cooked wax beans. Mr. Rider set his own plate on the piano bench, pushed aside the cardboard cartons of Grandma's letters and photo albums, and pulled the television forward into viewing range.

Daniel sat in a chair that was too comfortable for the way he felt. He wasn't used to being alone with his father.

"Shall we watch the news or a game show?" said Mr. Rider generously.

Do you remember when Mommy's sister Emma died? said Daniel in his mind, trying out a possible conversation.

"The news is bound to be rotten, but the game show would be worse."

Mommy was crying when she told me. I tried to be sad because I thought that's how you were supposed to be. I was only nine.

"There's always the eleven o'clock news I could catch, though, if you'd rather the game. It's a celebrity quiz or something."

I didn't really feel sad. More, I was excited about it. A real *thing* happening in our family. Mommy crying. Sarah crying. You holding Mommy in the front hall. Everybody coming for a party after the funeral.

"The news it is, then."

Did you feel nothing when Grandma died? The way I felt nothing when Aunt Emma died? But I was only nine.

"Lousy opening," said Mr. Rider. "Listen to that. Who writes this stuff, anyway?"

Daniel said to himself, *Say something.* Ask him about Grandma. What's holding you back? Just open your mouth and talk. *Talk.*

His fork skirted the wax beans, jabbed three french fries and a big chunk of hamburger, and carried the food up to his mouth. But his throat wouldn't swallow, so he sat through the evening news with food that he couldn't eat and words that he couldn't say.

Chapter Ten

For an entire week, nothing good happened at all.

Ed Gourney's unprovoked antagonism had increased, to the point where everyone in the school knew that he and Daniel were enemies. Jokes became jeers, and jeers became challenges. School was a miserable time of the day. The only good thing about it was that Susan was there. She continued to sit silently, looking asleep, doing her schoolwork impeccably.

And things were no better with Nikos. In fact, they were worse. The two or three brief conversations he'd had with Daniel had been the departing clarity before a storm of silence. He'd stopped shaving, and his face was being enveloped by the beard filling in.

"Some of them at choir practice think that it's just a matter of time," said Mrs. Rider.

"Till what?" said Daniel.

"Well . . . till his body follows the course his mind is taking."

"Till he dies," said Mr. Rider. "That's what they mean."

"But some of them say it's just grief taking its course

and folks don't die of grief. Old Alice Garvey thinks he should be taken to a hospital and hooked up to an IV. She's suggested it herself to Martha Phalen."

"I bet Martha loved that," said Mr. Rider.

"And Bob Karner thinks it's all a lot of mollycoddling, that Nikos shouldn't be allowed to stay at the Myer House. Self-indulgent, he says. Silly."

"Maybe he's right," said Mr. Rider.

"It's not silly," said Daniel, more to himself than to his father.

"All this attention on him just prolongs it," said Mr. Rider. "A minor situation blown all out of proportion."

But Daniel knew his father was wrong. The seriousness of the situation would be clear to Father August, surely; when Daniel explained it, Father August would know what to do. He'd be home by Good Friday; Nikos could hold on these last three weeks. He had to.

A week before Holy Thursday, Daniel and Susan stopped at the Myer House. Their conversations with Nikos had failed to do any good, since he was no longer answering, but they kept at it, unable to think of anything else to try.

Father Marston brought them a cup of hot chocolate in the living room. Nikos's eyes were focused, but not on anything apparent. Daniel and Susan sipped, and listened to each other sipping, and to the dripping of melting snow off the roof.

"Martha's off shopping; she'll be back later," said

Father Marston. "I'll be in the chapel readying for Stations if you need me, Daniel, Susan."

Daniel said tentatively, "Nikos, it must have been a terrible thing for you when Mark died."

Susan was stiff with nerves. They had discussed asking Nikos about the death of his friend; awkward though it would be for them, maybe Nikos just needed to talk about it. That's what Daniel had heard his mother saying to his father.

"Hmmm?" said Nikos.

"I said," gasped Daniel, trying again, "it must have been difficult for you when your friend died."

Nikos shook his head as if to clear his thoughts. But then he said nothing.

"Are you working on a new book of poetry?" said Susan.

"Or maybe a novel?" said Daniel, after a silence.

The winter sun came creamily in, its little warmth making them sleepy. Nikos rubbed his eyes and opened his mouth several times. Finally he said, "Thank you for coming to see me." And then he rose and blundered out of the room.

"Well, strike out once again for the team of Rider and Barrey," said Susan, making a face at the chocolate sludge in the bottom of the cup. "It's hardly worth our effort to come here, Daniel; he doesn't even recognize us."

"Sure he does. Of course it is. Don't say that. He just said thank you, that's more than he's said in days."

"One tiny hope in the face of all that nothingness."

"Well, at least there's something there." Daniel stretched back on the sofa, lazy from the sun. "We're not doing anything wonderful ourselves, Susan, of course not, how can we? But if we're just keeping our foot in the door, if we're keeping the door from slamming closed for good, then August can come and take our place. He and Nikos are friends."

"But what can he do? August isn't a miracle worker."

"He can talk to him. I don't know. They're friends. Something will happen."

"Something will happen to you if you don't get your feet off the good couch," said Mrs. Phalen, appearing at the doorway with paper bags. "What are you doing in here?"

"Father Marston gave us hot chocolate with Nikos." Daniel leaped up. "Mrs. Phalen, here's another loaf of bread my mother made and told me to bring to you. She doesn't think it's that bad."

"I'm sure it's lovely." Martha dropped her bags and took the bread. "She's making swift progress."

The front doorbell rang. Mrs. Phalen opened the door.

"I'm looking for my brother Nikos," said someone.

Daniel tapped Susan on the leg and motioned her to the hall.

"Well," said Martha Phalen. "Yes. Come right in. You're—"

"His sister," said the woman. "Filoretti O'Toole."

Filoretti stood uncertainly on the rug, snow melting off her white vinyl boots. Her long, dark hair was all frizzed out, and one hand kept busy by running itself through the curls.

"I'll call Father Marston," said Mrs. Phalen.

"I don't need any priest. I'm here to see my brother. He's still here?"

Mrs. Phalen hesitated, wondering if she should just let sisterly affection take its course. "Well, won't you sit down, and I'll go find Nikos," she said.

Filoretti O'Toole sat in a blue chair in the living room.

"Daniel, run round to the chapel and tell Father Marston what's happening," said Mrs. Phalen behind her hand. "Quick, now."

Daniel raced. Father Marston came with a swiftness of foot that surprised them both.

Nikos was just coming down the stairs when Daniel and Father Marston hurried in the front door. "Now, Nikos," said Father Marston, trying to catch his breath, "do you want—"

"There he is. Come in here, Nick," said Filoretti, rising from her chair.

"Perhaps we should withdraw," said Father Marston, beckoning Susan and Mrs. Phalen out of the room with a finger.

"I want to give you a thing or two," Filoretti said, "and say a word to you folks in charge here, so don't leave." She fumbled with the clasp on her large pocketbook, sprang it open, and drew out several piles of envelopes. "You've got creditors at every door for not paying bills that you owe," said Filoretti, holding up envelopes and fluttering statements at Nikos. "They've been coming to me as next of kin and I can't pay your bills, Nick. I've a hard enough time with my own. Your apartment in Albany has rent due for four months. I'm not going to be responsible. I'm *not* responsible. I want you to cross me off any form where it says next of kin."

Nikos looked stunned.

"Still a zombie, eh? Well, I'll just leave all this stuff here on the table and you can go through it later. If you ask me, you should be getting some professional help. You could write to the State Health Department, Nick, they'd give you some information, fill you in on things—"

"What?" Father Marston's smile faded. "What are you saying?"

"I'm his sister and I can't handle publishers and landlords and creditors calling me every day. There are institutions for people who are down and out like Nikos is now, and I'm just suggesting—"

"There's no need of that," said Father Marston.

"No sermon, Reverend." Filoretti pulled out a handkerchief and blew her nose. "Anything you could say has already occurred to me ten times over."

"You left him here weeks ago and haven't called once to see how he is," said Father Marston, his voice beginning to thunder. "Now you just come waltzing in here with big ideas; you've forfeited your right to lay down the law, Mrs.—"

"I'm laying down no laws. But can't you see I've had enough of him and the nonsense and the trouble? My boss is furious at all the office time I've spent on the phone with people calling about his bills. Don't you raise your voice to me when there's creditors at the door and bills piling up. I've tried to manage a bit, but there's no more I can do. I can't do it."

"Bills," said Mrs. Phalen, "bills, paperwork, we can handle. Just you leave it here and I'll tend to it. Nikos, why don't you and the kids go out for a walk—"

Sam Phalen appeared with a hammer in his hand.

"As long as I don't have to handle it, I don't care who does," said Filoretti sullenly. "All I want is not to be bothered about it. He was a smart kid, but look, he's crazy now. I can see it on his face."

"Trouble?" said Sam.

"I'll say trouble!" shouted Filoretti, at Sam, at Daniel and Susan, at Martha and Father Marston and Nikos. Beneath the sound of her anger rumbled the threat of tears. "Nothing but trouble for the past three months! Being so stupid as to let that Nesbitt freeze to death, and then mooning on and on about it like a schoolgirl, and me with my job and my Bob and my kids to take care of! He deserves being put away until he finds out what people have to be really crazy about. I wash my hands of him!" Filoretti slapped the sheaf of papers down on the coffee table. "Nothing but a silly schoolgirl."

"Enough," said Father Marston in his sermon voice. "Nikos has a home here for as long as he cares to stay, Mrs. O'Toole. Daniel took him in and he has a place here as long as he needs it. You can forward his mail to us. I will look at the papers and, if need be, speak to a lawyer about becoming the legal executor of your brother's business. You may rest assured of that."

"You're a fool. Feeling sorry for him. Pampering him. He's a fool. Blind and dumb. Good riddance to bad rubbish," said Filoretti. She blew her nose again and then angrily stuffed her crumpled handkerchief into her pocketbook.

Sam and Father Marston each took an elbow and led Filoretti out of the room. Martha Phalen stood stunned, looking after them. "Bad rubbish," she said, shaking, "bad rubbish."

She hurried to the front door. "Bad rubbish," she screamed at the top of her voice. "HOW DO YOU DARE?" She threw the loaf of Mrs. Rider's bread out the door at Filoretti.

Nikos Griskas seemed unaffected by the commotion. He wandered off in a daze.

"So what's so terrible about being a schoolgirl?" said Susan.

"Who knows?" said Daniel. "What's so terrible about being blind and dumb, when someone like that walks in the room."

"Now, Daniel," said Father Marston, returning to the front room, "the woman is distraught. Think of the shock of seeing her younger brother disintegrate before her eyes."

"That wasn't shock," said Mrs. Phalen, shaking so

violently that her husband put his arms around her. "It was sheer cruelty. Calling him *rubbish!*"

"I'm not so sure she was referring to him." Father Marston picked up the papers. "I'll look at these and see if I can make any sense of them."

Mrs. Phalen said fiercely, "We couldn't very well allow her to sign him into some overcrowded state institution where he'd never get the help and compassion he needs."

"Some institution where they are equipped to help him might be for the best," said Father Marston.

"He's here, he's staying here," said Martha, nodding in grim satisfaction.

"There!" said Mrs. Rider proudly.

Daniel and Mr. Rider surveyed the living room, which looked livable for the first time since the Riders had moved in at Christmas time. Some of Grandma's old furniture and fading photographs had been replaced by more familiar objects from the Riders' old apartment.

"Looks nice," said Mr. Rider.

"Now, don't be upset if anything important is missing; except for plain junk, I've packed your mother's things in boxes, which you can sort out at your leisure," said Mrs. Rider. "I haven't thrown anything away."

"No need to be so cautious," said Mr. Rider. "The place looks fine. You can throw the rest of the stuff out."

"Now, Bruce," said Mrs. Rider. "Your mother's things."

"They're only things. Let's not argue. You did a nice

job; the room is great. We should celebrate by having a party or something."

"A party! What a good idea," said Mrs. Rider. "We can ask Jason and Vera, and the Phalens, and I suppose Father Marston too, and maybe some of the choir members."

"A good way to show we're feeling settled here," said Mr. Rider.

Who feels settled? thought Daniel.

"And you can ask some friends too, Daniel; how about Susan Barrey?" Mrs. Rider seemed overly enthusiastic. "And that boy, the one who goes with Jason on his deliveries?"

"No, not him," said Daniel. And, after a pause, he said firmly, "I'll ask Nikos."

"Oh, I don't know—" said Mrs. Rider.

"Well, why not?" said Mr. Rider. "I've never seen the fellow. Maybe it would do him some good to be invited out."

"I'll make several loaves of my best bread," said Mrs. Rider. "I'll call Father Marston right away. Bruce, would you start a salad for dinner?"

Mrs. Rider came into the kitchen a few minutes later. Daniel was setting the table elaborately, folding the napkins so they stood upright, using the good silver with the rose design. Mr. Rider shredded lettuce and rinsed it in the sink, with great splashing.

"Father Marston said that the church suggests a community meal on Holy Thursday," said Daniel's mother, "and they ask that people of the parish meet in various homes and eat together, as commemoration of the Last Supper. He said he and the Phalens and maybe Nikos Griskas would come, and even Father Petrakis if he's home by then, on Thursday evening after the services at St. Mark's. A bring-and-share supper, he called it. And people will be meeting like that all over the parish."

"Fine," said Mr. Rider.

"Oh, I *hope* Father August will come." Daniel realized that the whole next week would be saturated with wishing his friend would be there.

"Time will tell. Father Marston said not to count on Nikos's coming, though. He'd suggest it but couldn't guarantee anything. Goodness, Daniel, the table looks as good as a restaurant."

Daniel beamed.

The phone rang during dinner. "Honey, it's for you," said Daniel's mother. Mr. Rider grunted, pushed his chair away from the table, and reached for the phone.

"All right, elephant ears," said Mrs. Rider, "if your father wants you to know who it is, he'll tell you when he comes back to the table. Now, how was school today?"

"Okay," said Daniel.

But Mr. Rider didn't come back to the table to finish his meal. "Bad news," he called in from the hall, jingling his keys. "That was Father Marston. Nikos has disappeared."

"What!" Daniel and his mother spoke in one voice.

"He just seems to have vanished. Damn fool. Guess

there was some sort of commotion there today, his sister came by or something. Father Marston says Nikos has been in a daze for some time. Maybe the sister took him away."

"Well, that would be understandable," said Mrs. Rider.

"She wouldn't do that," said Daniel.

"But in case she didn't, Father Marston is rounding up some men to go out and search for him. He might have wandered anywhere. His coat and boots are still at the Myer House, Father Marston said, so he's unprotected."

"Oh, Lord," said Mrs. Rider. "Well, at least it's warmer out than it has been. He won't freeze to death."

Mr. Rider pulled on his coat. "Well, just pray that he didn't wander out on the ice. It's not safe now."

"You're not going out looking for him," said Mrs. Rider.

"Well, there's certainly no reason why I should. If he's incompetent enough to get lost in the hills, he deserves what's coming to him. Sensible folk being called from their dinner tables. He ought to be fined."

What a joke, thought Daniel, him clomping around like some big-hearted neighbor when there's really nothing inside but disdain.

"I'll come with you," said Daniel.

"No, you won't," said Mr. Rider.

"Absolutely not," said Mrs. Rider. "You'll stay here, safe. I know he's your friend, but nothing would be helped by your getting lost too." She jumped to her feet and pulled off her apron. "I'll come with you, Bruce."

"Now, Marion, that's just as silly—"

"Can the nonsense, Bruce, and get your boots on. Nikos is still young enough to be my son. Where're we meeting the others?"

"At the Myer House. Marion, none of the other wives will be out tramping in the woods—"

"So, let them bake their perfect breads and I'll tramp in the woods. Daniel, if you feel like doing the dishes, go ahead, but you don't have to."

"It's not fair!" said Daniel.

"Nothing is," said Mrs. Rider, "but I'm your mother and I say no and that's how it goes. Daniel, we'll call the minute anything happens, at least as quickly as we can get to a phone. Bruce, are you ready? I imagine we'll start in the village and search the obvious places first—"

"Max Grober's coming in on his snowmobile, so he'll be looking out in the fields," said Mr. Rider. "Goodbye, Daniel." He kissed him absentmindedly.

"Don't be angry at us," said Mrs. Rider. She kissed him. And his parents bustled out, scarves and flashlights and concern rattling them.

The mountains? Would Nikos just walk up in the mountains at night? Or did Filoretti come back and kidnap him? But why would she do that? Or maybe, maybe— did he wander out on the ice and fall through, the way Daniel himself had fallen through?

He called Susan immediately.

She was in tears.

"So you've heard about Nikos being lost," said Daniel soberly.

"It's not Nikos I'm upset about!" cried Susan. "It's Papa. Mr. Grober came from next door to borrow some snowshoes, and Papa hadn't gone to bed yet, and the whole story about Nikos came out while I was upstairs hunting for the snowshoes. I come down, and Papa's shuffling around like a little mouse, pulling on my red-and-green mittens and his old plaid coat and earmuffs, and nothing Mr. Grober or I could say would stop him. I haven't seen him move so well—ever. It's shocking. In the end I saw him ride off on the back of Mr. Grober's snowmobile, and I can't believe it."

Daniel didn't know what to say.

"It's not as if he even has any idea who Nikos Griskas is," said Susan. "He just remembers doing this in the past. Someone needs help. So off he goes. And there was no room for me on the snowmobile, so here I am, stuck and useless, like a baby."

"Well, me too."

"Do you think it was Filoretti? Do you think she came and stole her brother?"

"I doubt it. But it wouldn't actually be stealing, would it, since she's his sister?"

Susan was silent. After a minute she said, "You know him better than the rest of us do. Where do you think he is?"

"I don't know," said Daniel. He was afraid to say what he thought.

Chapter Eleven

The night dragged on. Daniel did the dishes, wrapped up the uneaten food, alternating chores with dashes to the window to see if anyone was coming.

His bedtime came and passed. He couldn't go to sleep.

For a while he stared out the windows at the dark, icy lake. It had seemed so kind, such a comfort, the water in the autumn and the ice in winter reaching right up, just thirty yards from the house. But tonight it seemed menacing, alien; the ice gleamed like aluminum foil in the black night, and who knew whether or not the ice would yield, would buckle, would fold its hands underwater at last, leaving anyone who'd been standing in its palms to drown and freeze?

You couldn't freeze in the night air, not tonight, thought Daniel. It's too warm, it's like a spring night almost. But you would freeze if you were folded into the lake.

Around the house the rushing of melting water sounded.

The house was still, ominous. All the furniture in the living room seemed about to pounce. The pictures on the wall seemed suspended just by the tension of the night;

when the tension reached its climax, the whole world would shudder.

Daniel clawed a rip in the sofa, out of fear, when a shelf of ice slid off the porch roof and thudded terribly in the bushes.

To calm himself, to pass the time, he sat down at the boxes of things that had belonged to his grandmother, and he searched through them.

Yellowing photographs, letters, ribbons and ticket stubs, bills of sale, programs from concerts. A few buttons on a strip of lace. At the bottom of the first box was an old dried twig in a funny shape.

Daniel took it out. It was formed like a man, a man with one leg straight and the other bent. It looked like a dancer, a harlequin in bark. Daniel stood it up against the piano.

The phone rang. It was Susan, nervous, news-less.

When Daniel sat back down on the rug near the man, he remembered the time around Thanksgiving when he had spent two weeks with his grandmother, just before she died. They had sat in this room, in front of the fireplace, talking about the mountains and the neighbors and many things.

And all that was left was this funny, twiggy man, and Grandma wasn't even around to say what it meant or where she'd found it . . .

He sat in her old rocker to see if there was any feeling of her left there. But what there was was only feeling. "Are you still around?" he said quietly. "Are you somewhere near?"

All he heard was the drip of melting snow off the eaves.

He went back to the letters. Would she want me reading these, he wondered for a minute. Certainly I wouldn't want anyone looking at my notebook or letters if I were dead. But the only alternative, worrying about Nikos, was too consuming.

After he opened the second letter, he felt justified.

Dated 1943, the letter from Carolyn Rider was addressed to her husband, Benjamin, who was stationed in England. Most of it was news about people in Canaan Lake, and about their two children, Bruce and Sharon. Daniel skipped a lot of it. But one part at the end read:

After services on Thursday morning, I was walking home along the lake road and I found a twig, not far from Aunt Ruth's place. I was thinking about the time you and I went out riding unescorted, when we were courting, and we were much later returning than we'd planned, because of the mare's bad knee. How furious Aunt Ruth was! The accusations and the unpleasantness that followed, senselessly—and then she died before we'd ever been reconciled. For several years I've harbored a resentment of Aunt Ruth, for her hard ways. But lately I've been thinking that I must forgive Aunt Ruth her harshness, even though she's dead. I must forgive the past—and let it be past. Perhaps I must be for-given by it, too. Forgiven and released.

So this twig, Ben, it looks like a man, a leaping man; and I took it up in my hands with the same interest I used to feel as a child receiving a birthday present. I took it home, and it is standing on the mantel. I'm not one for superstition, as you know, but even as I held it the first time the odd notion came to me: this is an image of the resurrected Saviour. So there he leaps, Ben, on the mantel, made of wood but freed from the cross—the uncrucified Christ. The ultimate release of the past: death itself breaking its chains.

Forgive my sounding preachy, Ben! It's no habit I expect to encourage. But that twig took a special hold on me, and in a private way I respect what it represents to me. When you come home you will see it. I am im-patient for you to return; I'm lonely (there, I've said it), even with Bruce and Sharon around me all the time . . .

Lonely? Grandma lonely? Even with her two children around her?

Daniel took the twig in his hand—it was leaping like an Olympic gymnast—and he twirled it between his palms as if he were rolling ropes of modeling clay. The figure slowly spun around like a dancer rotating on top of a fancy music box.

Oh, Nikos, forgive the past, like Grandma said. Let it be past.

He put the other letters back in the box and took the Christ and the 1943 letter up to his room. He stood the twig on the windowsill, and he folded the letter in the book of Nikos's poems. The photograph of Nikos smiled glossily up from the back cover.

Oh, Lord, save him, said Daniel. He wasn't even sure if that qualified as a prayer, being so short and obvious, but it was all he could think of.

The sound of scattering slush jolted him. There was a car in the driveway. As he ran downstairs, he saw the time on the hall clock: midnight.

"Tea, tea," said Mrs. Rider wearily.

"What happened?"

"Oh, Daniel, I thought you'd be asleep by now—"

"WHAT HAPPENED?"

"Don't you shout at your mother. She's been out trekking in the woods . . ."

Daniel was almost in tears.

"Nothing happened, Daniel." Mrs. Rider collapsed on the kitchen bench and tried to kick off her boots. Dirty water spun out all over the floor. "No luck. No clues. Nobody found him."

"And almost the whole town turned out," said Mr. Rider. "Considering that most folk don't even know him, it was surprising."

"Well, you don't know him, Bruce, and you tramped all the way up to Pine Slide in the dark," said Mrs. Rider. Mr. Rider put on the kettle.

"I should have come," said Daniel.

"Oh, Daniel. We looked everywhere."

"Well, where can he be? He can't be nowhere."

"Lord knows where he is. Father Marston tried all night to reach that sister in Glens Falls by phone. He even had the state police involved. She couldn't be located."

"I saw your friend's grandfather—old Isaac Barrey," said Mr. Rider, depositing his scarf in a wet heap. "Thought he'd kill himself, jolting around on the back of the Grobers' snowmobile. He wouldn't be pried off. And Max Grober said he was a help, too; he remembered some of the trails through the abandoned orchards up west of the cemetery."

"We looked in all the village buildings," said Mrs. Rider, "in St. Mark's and in Vera's boardinghouse, and the post office and Meister's. Woke up a good many people ringing their bells."

"And we covered all the lower slopes of the hills," said Mr. Rider. "Calling for him till we were hoarse. When he's found he ought to be whipped."

"But we didn't venture out on the ice," said Mrs. Rider. "Jason and Vera drove around the lake, stopping every hundred yards or so, and shining heavy-duty searchlights out onto the ice, to see signs of breakage or footprints. But of course they couldn't go traipsing out on the ice. Jason says it's much too close to breaking. Thank you, Daniel— would you just grab the sugar—and Father Marston says that in the daylight we should be able to see a body—"

"No!" said Daniel.

"—if there is a body. Don't get excited; this is just conjecture now. If it's at all questionable, they'll get a small plane to fly over the lake looking for him."

"Was there a mist tonight?" asked Daniel weakly.

"Oh, it's warm and steamy," said Mrs. Rider. "Warm enough for mist. So he won't freeze, Daniel, no worry of that. Now don't you think you should get up to bed? I promise I'll wake you if we hear anything, though most of the searchers have gone home for the night."

"Jason Meister and Sam Phalen are still out," said Mr. Rider. "They were just setting out to take a look up on the slopes of the Two Sisters when we came in." His brow was set in a way Daniel had never seen before. The harsh light of the kitchen, foreign in the middle of the night, made his father seem a stranger in his own home. Daniel couldn't bring himself to kiss this stranger good night, though he felt a grudging gratitude to him for searching for Nikos.

And then he couldn't sleep.

His parents had settled down an hour ago, and the house had been still but for the constant rush of melted snow sliding and dripping and skimming outside. He lay in his bed, in the funny striped nightshirt, and the room was thick with shadow and fear. Then he threw aside his blankets and ran to the window, sure that he would see, out on the ice, Nikos or the mist or *something*. But the lake reached off into the ominous night, and Nikos was still lost in it.

"He's not capable of finding his way back," said Daniel aloud, arguing the point, surprising himself.

There was a sound like baseball cards flipping on bicycle spokes, and then, skittering, hovering, repeating taps on the glass, the bird with the firelit eyes was suddenly there.

"Come in," said Daniel, yanking up the window. "Are you going to lead me to Nikos?"

The bird didn't settle tonight. It flapped convulsively around the room, scratching and stalling on the headboard of Daniel's bed, and then launching itself again.

"All right," whispered Daniel, reaching for the feather underneath his pillow, "I'm ready, I guess. Not asleep at all, but ready if you want to be going."

The bird arched its wings; Daniel held the feather forward. The same astonishing procedure: Daniel flew out the window after the bird, the warmish wind like ribbons between his toes.

But tonight the bird sought no altitude. It dove and swooped around the corner of the Rider house, close to the shadows and the aroma of the conifers, over the front-porch roof: into the window of his parents' room.

No, said Daniel in his mind.

The bird began to settle into the dream in the room, the dream of Daniel's father.

No, no, said Daniel, beginning to struggle, kicking, even as the dream mouthed his ankles, no!

His father turned in the darkness, murmured, was still; the bird hesitated on the borderline of dream.

No, said Daniel once more. If I have to scream and wake them up, I will, I swear it. I don't want to see my father's dreams.

The bird was not deaf to Daniel's earnest protests. It waved its wings and pulled Daniel out of the room.

They soared. The night like strange warm milk poured past. Beneath them the sheet of lake ice was the color of silver ash, from the village at the southwest end to the rounded cove eight miles north. But they were so high that Daniel could see no crack in the ice where Nikos might have fallen through, no dark smudge that might be a collapsed body.

The bird began to sink, down toward the dark fringe of the lakes's north shore, and Daniel followed. For a few minutes he couldn't quite orient himself, coming upon things at these new angles. But he realized with a shudder that the bird was zeroing in on the squat stone house that belonged to Susan's grandfather. With a spurt of speed— as if to prevent Daniel's having time to resist—the bird dipped and leveled, and passed through the glass of the living-room window. And Daniel followed.

The room was dark, except for a small night-light; a heavy, gurgling breath rippled the shadows. The dream, strung along the breath, was tattered and worried. As its fingers closed over Daniel, he saw, for just a few seconds, old exhausted Papa, asleep on the couch, with two chairs pushed up to the edge to keep him from falling off. Susan's red-and-green mittens were pulled onto the upright posts of one of the chairs to dry. Two woolen hands in the darkness, palms out, opposed.

And then Daniel was in Papa's dream.

Such as it was. Jason's dream had been a cacophony of segments. Papa's was simple. Papa was dreaming about himself, asleep on the sofa, waiting to die.

This went on for some time, with little variation. Daniel began to be impatient. He wanted to wander around in the dream, looking at things, but there was nothing else. Just Papa himself, breathing in and out with a noise like a steam engine, asleep on the sofa and expecting death.

After a while Daniel thought: It's odd that he isn't very frightened of it.

Maybe that thought provoked the dream.

There was a church. It was St. Mark's, in the town of Canaan Lake. There were chores to be done. Papa was a young man walking in the emerald grass of early morning, with a stepladder on his shoulder. Good morning, Father, he said to the vicar. Then he put his ladder to the front of the church and climbed all the way up to the wooden cross at the peak of the roof.

He had a brush. He painted the cross white. The organist in the church was practicing. Isaac sang along, catching the drips with the edge of his brush. *In Christ there is no East or West,* sang Isaac. When the next chorus came around, he sang the version that someone, very drunk, had once belted out one Sabbath. *In Christ there is no Feast or Rest.* Then the organist began practicing scales.

The dream fluttered, insubstantial.

Isaac was on a snowmobile in the orchards. Looking for someone. The orchards were thick with slush and the machine caught on patches of mud. A ghostly light pushed down from the misty skies. Then it was a horse he was riding, down a long arcade whose ice-laden branches jingled overhead like harness bells. If the young lost one is dead, thought Isaac, why is it him and not me?

A large, featureless woman stood on the newly built porch of the stone house. The porch was still unsanded and unpainted, and the woman's bare feet were likely to pick up splinters. Come on in, then, silent Isaac, said the woman, and eat you some supper.

Isaac ate some supper. The woman bore a baby son, and then she died.

Why her and not me, said Isaac, cradling the ugly baby. A baby should have a mother.

Again the dream lost its grip. The thread fell slack.

It's not, said Isaac, as if I've much to give to a baby.

Isaac was cleaning the Stations of the Cross with brass cleaner. The smell was horrific. On Station number six, Veronica Wipes the Face of Jesus, young Isaac Barrey wiped the face of Veronica with a rag, and Veronica's whole head came off. Faulty craftsmanship, he said to the vicar. But you have to pay, said the vicar.

I'm tired of paying, said Isaac.

Where's the rest for the weary? Where's the balm?

Life has been, on the whole, rather empty, said Isaac. But I've stuck it out. Now where's my reward?

But there was no knock on the door, no fluttering of angel wings. There was just Isaac Barrey on the couch, sleeping.

Daniel Rider was more aware of himself in the thinness of this dream than he'd been in Jason's. He felt uncomfortable, suspicious of Papa's calling for death, suspicious of the curious lack of intensity in the dream. Why had the bird brought him here?

A flag of dream still fluttered.

Isaac was on the snowmobile. This time he was sitting behind the big warm back of Max Grober. Isaac was pointing out the old trails, the breaks in stone walls, the forgotten roads. Cold was gripping old Isaac's thumbs. But he wasn't complaining to Max about the cold. He was pressing his thumbs into his palms to keep them warm. After all, someone was lost out here, out in the hinterlands, no matter how empty life was. A baby needed to be brought up.

Then the dream ran out of steam. Daniel emerged, unsatisfied, staring for a minute at Papa's sunken face, lit by the glow of the little lemon-yellow night-light plugged into the wall. His jaw had fallen open and his breathing was easier. Hard to believe those little hands broke off the head of poor St. Veronica.

The bird hopped to an arm of the couch, near old Isaac's head. A tip of one wing came out, almost as if to brush the alabaster smoothness of Isaac's brow.

Then the wings whipped and the bird tore away.

Good night, Papa, said Daniel in his mind, as he lunged off after his guide.

They raced back, and Daniel had scarcely settled his feet on the floor of his room when the bird was gone again, frantic wings stirring the night.

He got in his bed and pulled the covers up, puzzled at the night's dream.

Then he remembered that Papa was the second choice; the bird had led him to his father's dream first, and he had rejected it. What had his father's dream been about?

He sat up.

Jason in the first dream, longing for dead Alma; Papa in the second dream, waiting for death; could the bird be explaining to him about death? Could it be because, maybe, Nikos had died tonight? And these excursions had been lessons, preparing Daniel for a tragedy of immense impact?

Had his father been dreaming about death? Whose?

And then he couldn't sleep, of course, for the rest of the night.

When the sky brightened to the color of weak tea, Daniel dressed and went downstairs with his journal. He sat in the chilly kitchen and didn't think of breakfast.

He wrote down as much as he could remember of the two dreams. Someday he might forget them, and in a journal there would be clues, reminders, some description, however imperfect, that he could rely on. I can't forget what's happened these days, ever, ever, Daniel wrote.

Dreams and bird and everyone's eyes wide at the thought of death.

Mrs. Rider came downstairs a while later, yawning. She plugged in the electric coffeepot, and its steam melted the frost on the kitchen window. The lake outside was grim; the mountains around it bare and lonely.

Oh, what a lonely world, Daniel wrote, not knowing exactly why.

"Homework?" said Mrs. Rider.

"No."

"Oh." She didn't seem very concerned. She sat down at the table, folded her houserobe close about her, and cracked her knuckles. "One thing I really miss about Manhattan is home delivery of the newspapers. I can't get used to reading *Newsweek* with my morning coffee, or an old Sunday *Times.*"

Daniel slammed his notebook shut. "Any news would be something," he said, "just so we'd *know.*"

"Well, we'll have to live with whatever happens, you know," said his mother. "Even if it's something terrible. And time heals all wounds."

"I don't believe that," said Daniel stubbornly.

"I never did either," said Mrs. Rider. "I don't even know why I just said it." She got up. "Have you had something to eat?"

"No, thanks, I'm not hungry."

"You have to eat something, Daniel, don't be silly." She poured some cold cereal in a bowl and cut up a rather soft banana in it. "I didn't sleep well at all."

"I didn't sleep at all, period."

"You'll be sorry in school today—"

Mrs. Rider dropped a banana in the sink and Daniel knocked his notebook on the floor as they both scrambled to answer the phone. It rang just once. Their cold hands met on the receiver, and Mrs. Rider wrestled it to her ear. "Hello? Hello?"

Daniel's breath caught in his throat; he was a small column of organic matter whose life was suspended—

"Oh. Oh." Mrs. Rider's hand went out, caught Daniel's neck. "Oh." There was a pause. "Oh."

The sky lightened from the color of weak tea, a degree or two.

"Well. Thank God," said Mrs. Rider.

Life released itself back into Daniel, rushing with such intensity that it flooded his ears and clouded his eyes, and his mother was standing there, looking at him, the receiver back on its hook, before he knew it.

"Jason and Sam found him out on the ice," said Mrs. Rider. "They searched all night. That was Martha. They dared the ice to go out and get him. He's not dead. He was even talking, Martha said, mumbling about some lights. Jason and Vera are driving him right down to Glens Falls General Hospital. Thank God for an unseasonably warm night!" She hugged Daniel suddenly, fiercely. "This is cause for a good hot cup of coffee. No better way to celebrate it." She turned to the coffeepot and said over her shoulder, "You want some?"

"Yes," said Daniel.

"Wait a minute, what am I saying? You're not old enough to drink coffee yet." But she poured him a cup.

"Besides, I've had it before," said Daniel gratefully, babbling. "Grandma used to serve it to me sometimes. Should we wake up Daddy and tell him Nikos is found?"

"No, let him sleep, poor man. He was tossing and groaning all night, mumbling in his sleep. Bad dreams too, I bet. Let him sleep."

"Hurray, hurray," said Daniel, uncontrollable.

Chapter Twelve

"Absolutely not," said Mrs. Rider.

"But if I left right now, in a few minutes, there'd be plenty of time," said Daniel. Even as he talked he was reaching for his boots. He wanted to walk to school instead of waiting for the bus.

"If you've had no sleep at all, you'll only exhaust yourself," said his mother.

"It'll invigorate me. Look, the sun's out, it's going to be a beautiful day. I've got tons of time. You're spilling the coffee, Mommy."

"I see that," said his mother crossly. "Well, don't you go calling me up in the middle of the day wanting to come home, because I won't come and get you. I'm going to be at the Myer House looking over some of their records. I don't want to be disturbed."

"I won't call you. Promise." He rushed out.

As if to celebrate Nikos's being found, the world was suddenly reeking with spring. A skin of water covered everything; puddles, rivulets, melting snow, and dripping icicles. The world was shiny in its waterskin. Daniel smiled at his reflection in the puddles. He wanted, suddenly, to take a boat out on the lake and look for his reflection in the water.

He plunged through the brush to the lake. He slipped on the stripes of mud and slush, falling to one knee and covering his leg with mud.

The ice at the edge of the lake was gone, its cold touch pulled back. A few inches of water showed, a grainy ribbon of lake. Daniel laughed and splashed himself. Things would be all right.

Straightening up, he looked out across the lake.

Just beginning to glow, the mystifying lights appeared. It was the first time Daniel had seen them actually arrive. They didn't rise out of the lake or descend out of the air, or even move forward from the triangular rise of mountain behind them. They didn't displace or intrude upon anything that was already there. They materialized entirely independently of the buoyant spring day.

It was not a metamorphosis of normal things into magical. It was an arrival of light, Daniel saw now, that had no parentage in Canaan Lake. It was really coming from nowhere.

He stood still and watched.

Once again, the values of light seemed engaged in assuming some pattern. It's like staring at a fire, thought Daniel. After a while you begin to think the flames are struggling to imitate something, to achieve some recognizable form, and who knows that they're not?

The light arranged itself into the vaguely striped arrangement: vertical bands of clouded and unshadowed mist. Again Daniel thought of pillars, of a vast illuminated crowd of pillars coming to birth at the edge of Canaan Lake.

With a jolt, Daniel realized that he was seeing something else, too, and scarcely understanding it: there was now a depth of field to the lights. The shimmering columns were not lined up all in a row, as columns of a temple would be. Instead, they were at varying random distances, like cornstalks in a field, and the ones in the center were closest.

Daniel's eyes squinted at the nearest columns, eager, desperate for some detail or clue. Surely he'd be able to see something—

—he saw something—

—and the scream that came out of his mouth turned the lights back, because the lights began to fade, by degrees. Even before the sound of the scream had faded, the lights were gone again.

"Oh, Father August," cried Daniel, "come on *home!*"

He scrambled back to Route 103 and began running toward the school. For fifteen minutes he ran, till a cramp bit at his side and he had to slow to a walk.

In the face of what he had seen, what he had realized, an army of rational impulses came surging to the surface. You're tired, said the army, you've been up all night, you've been having strange dreams, you've been worried about Nikos Griskas, and maybe your eyes aren't all that reliable anyway.

I know what I saw, pumped the heart in Daniel.

You've an overactive imagination, said the rational debator in him.

I know what I saw, throbbed the heart, repetitious, irrefutable.

Now wait, said Daniel to himself, stilling the heart and calming the logic. Even if I saw what I think I saw, there's no reason to be so petrified. I know that odd things happen to me. It's just my way of knowing things. Other people—like Father August—can know things just by listening and thinking. I know them by this funny magic, and maybe everyone has their own magic things happening to them. It's almost normal for these things to happen to me. This isn't the first time. So why get upset?

What's so upsetting, anyway, about columns of light shimmering above an icy lake, stilling the pulse of time whenever they appear? What's so upsetting about the fact that the nearest column is not strictly columnar, but has a rounded top and minor swells and dips in its sides? What is so chilling about the fact that, for whatever reason, the column of light breaking into the fabric of the world resembles, more or less, a human being?

"What's wrong?" said Susan.

"Lots and lots," said Daniel out of the corner of his mouth.

"Page 76," said the teacher. "Numbers 1 through 20. Complete sentences of course. To be handed in at the end of the period. Get working."

"Nikos?" whispered Susan.

"He's been found," said Daniel.

"No talking, please," said the teacher.

"Write it down," suggested Susan.

"A question, Miss Barrey?"

"No, sir."

The class was still. The teacher settled down at his desk and began to correct papers. Daniel opened the text. The questions were not hard. He answered them in complete sentences, quickly. Everyone else was referring to the book for clues; Daniel was the first finished.

He closed his textbook and drew his journal up to the desktop. He rarely brought it to school for fear of its being taken, like Harriet the Spy's; all kinds of terrible things could happen then. But he'd been so upset by Nikos that he'd abandoned caution. He had to write these things down.

His printing, usually small and elegant, flowed out today in a leaning scrawl. The strange dream of Papa's; Nikos being found on the ice by Sam and Jason; the terrible humanness of the lights on the lake. It feels like a moment in history, wrote Daniel, like some key event is approaching that will change everything. Like the difference between B.C. and A.D. Are Susan and I the only ones who know it?

"I'll have that." The teacher was standing over him.

"But—"

"This is work time, not play time."

"But—I finished my work, look, all twenty."

The teacher took the notebook, just as if it were any old notebook and didn't have a secret of the world in it, and he strolled back to his desk. "You should have gone on to the next chapter."

"But you didn't say to." Daniel's voice broke.

"I'm saying it now. And you ought to have known. Proper study habits are the most important thing you can learn from us, Rider."

Daniel detested, beyond all else, being called by just his last name. He hated it so much that, for a precious few seconds, he was consumed with loathing for the teacher. And then the last possible moment was past for him to have anything to say—

"I object," rang out Susan's voice. The class, to a person, came alive. The teacher looked up with a fake innocence on his face, as if he couldn't possibly imagine what Susan was objecting to.

"That's just plain thievery," said Susan, folding her hands on her desk, her eyes—yes, they really were, noted Daniel—flashing.

"Miss Barrey?" said the teacher, as if they'd just been introduced. "You have a comment?"

"You don't have any right to Daniel Rider's notebook. If you don't want him looking at it, you can tell him to put it away. But you didn't give him any further assignment yet, so he wasn't disobeying you, so you don't have any right to take it from him."

"You have an interest, perhaps, in what Daniel Rider's

notebook contains?" said the teacher. The class laughed. The teacher smiled.

"That's not the point," said Susan.

Daniel couldn't believe it. A battle going on over his private notebook. And he wasn't even one of the warriors. He'd never have had the nerve to speak up. Trust Susan!

The teacher stood up suddenly, and the smile left his face. Business now, and tough business. "Miss Barrey," he said, "you've been in this school since September. That's long enough to know that we don't tolerate being lectured to by our students. Would you step out in the hall, please."

Susan walked unflinchingly to the door. She disappeared without looking at anyone. The teacher followed. The door stayed open. The rest of the class gritted their teeth and leaned forward in an effort to hear what the teacher was saying to Susan.

And then the oddest thing happened.

Ed Gourney, villain of the class, was out of his seat, on his toes, moving in long, silent steps down the aisle. He jostled Daniel's elbow as he went by. Daniel was about to retort sharply, when Ed Gourney reached the teacher's desk. He snatched up Daniel's notebook and laid down one of his own in its place. The class was mesmerized at this outrage. Ed Gourney stole quickly back. Passing Daniel's desk, he said, "You're kind of a fool, you know," and dropped the notebook there. Daniel scooped it into his desk. And then the teacher and Susan came back in.

"Continue, 21 through 30," said the teacher grimly. Susan walked to her desk, her face flushed. Daniel wanted to catch her eye, to let her know that a rescue had occurred. But she just went back to work. The whole class went back to work.

Allies in strange places, thought Daniel, and began on number 21.

Just before lunch the teacher gave Daniel back the substitute notebook. "So you were working at Mr. Gourney's science notes. Lord alone knows why—you won't learn anything from him." Oh, yeah? said Daniel to himself. "In the future, keep to the assignment, Rider. Understand?"

"Yes, sir."

"Good. Dismissed."

Susan was waiting around the corner for him. "You got it back," she said, "and do you think he looked at it?"

"He did," said Daniel. "Come on, I have to give this back, right away."

"Give it back?"

They hurried down the stairs to the din of the cafeteria. Daniel walked boldly up to the table where Ed Gourney reigned and handed him his notebook. Susan hung back a little, perplexed.

"Thanks for your help," said Daniel.

"It wasn't so much to help you as to foil him," said Ed Gourney in a public way, speaking to his throng as well as to Daniel.

"Well, you foiled him and I got my notebook back, so thanks."

"Your friend Susan was pretty interested in what you have in that notebook," said Ed, working for a laugh.

"So would you be," said Daniel shortly.

They looked at each other for a minute, not smiling. But that was all right. No smiles were needed.

After they'd filled up their trays with the daily supplies of Coke and Cheese Twists, Daniel and Susan sat down, and Susan learned about what had happened. She raised an eyebrow at the story of Ed Gourney's rescue. She leaned on the table to get every word of the story of Papa's dream. And she was relieved to hear of Nikos's survival.

"I think you ought to lend me the feather for the weekend," she said. "I want to go flying to other people's dreams. After all, I was there the day the bird flew out of the mist."

"All right." Daniel felt generous. Susan's loyalty deserved repayment. And it was nice, for the first time in five weeks, to be able to sit in the cafeteria and talk, and not be the audience for a chanting chorus of Ed Gourney's cronies. The chorus was silent today.

Chapter Thirteen

But the bird didn't come to Susan's window. On Monday morning she had to say reluctantly to Daniel that she had slept soundly and undisturbed. "But I always sleep soundly and undisturbed," she admitted.

"That's no surprise to me," said Daniel, and when she offered it he took the feather back.

Daniel had called the Myer House. Father Marston had told him that Nikos was still under surveillance at the hospital down in Glens Falls. "But he's not hurt," reassured the priest. "They just want to be sure he doesn't contract pneumonia. A few days and he'll be back."

"Get off the phone, Daniel, there's work to be done," said Mrs. Rider. "If a houseful of guests is descending on Thursday, we'd better start the show on the road. Baseboards first."

"Oh, Mommy." This was a standard argument of Daniel's: he saw no reason to dust baseboards. The way his mother talked, clean baseboards were the requirement for any entertaining. But Daniel knew that only in his imagination would stalky Vera Meister trot into the living room, her big plastic beads rattling around her neck, to heave aside the sofa, run a gloved finger up and down the baseboards, and sniff, "Really, Marion! Dust! I've a good mind to go right home."

Daniel began to recite this scenario, out of habit. His mother handed him a rag without listening.

Daniel flipped the rag on the beveling. Gee, it was dusty. He felt strangely, privately glad that the black bird had not taken Susan to someone's dreams. The sun strove to warm the living room, the dust that Daniel flicked away went dancing in the yellowness. "Remember, Man, that thou art dust," he sang, the old-fashioned words sounding grander than the newer version, "and unto dust thou shalt return."

"Well, the hospital sent Nikos back to the Myer House," said Mrs. Rider as she walked with Daniel to the car. "They told Father Marston that there wasn't much more they could do for him; specialists down in Albany might be better trained to prescribe some treatment."

"I wonder if he'll come tonight?" said Daniel.

"Daniel, do you have a handkerchief? I wonder if three loaves of bread is enough. I hope it's good. It looked a little solid to me. Did you set out the wineglasses, the good ones?"

"Yes, I do," said Daniel. "Yes, I did."

"You do what?" said his mother.

"Have a handkerchief. Set out the wineglasses. Why isn't Daddy coming?"

"He doesn't come to these things. You know that."

"If I have to, why doesn't he have to?"

"Daniel! I thought you liked church."

"I do. Usually." And he did, though it was one of those things he didn't broadcast on the school bus. He liked things being solemn and orderly. He liked the idea of God moving in mysterious ways. When he was younger he thought that meant God moved on a railroad car with wings, for instance, or in a helicopter with big hen's feet sticking out of the bottom like a Baba Yaga house. Now he didn't know *what* it meant; people like August did know, probably. He didn't care. He still liked the mysteriousness of vestments and apostles and angels and flaming swords. He liked the fact that there was a place such as church even on Sundays when he didn't feel much like going.

"You're distracting me. Why doesn't Daddy come?"

"He says his prayers in his own way," said Mrs. Rider. "I think he'd do better to attend service regularly, but I won't chide him. He's more familiar with the Bible than either of us."

"You'd never know it." That was a bona fide mutter.

"For shame! On Holy Thursday! I heard that! You're not too big to be spanked, you know!"

Daniel thought perhaps he was, but didn't argue the matter.

St. Mark's was packed. Daniel sat on the inside end of a pew, where he could lean up against the wall and rest his head while Father Marston delivered his sermon.

His mind wandered. Daniel could see Susan off on the

other side of the church, sitting ramrod straight, and beside her, his neck swathed in plaid flannel, Papa. How many times in his life has he attended Holy Thursday service, Daniel wondered idly, picking threads from his coat and twirling them like tiny jump ropes.

"Pay attention," breathed Mrs. Rider, admonition hissing in the whisper.

"Are you and Papa coming over for some bring-and-share supper?" said Daniel to Susan after the service.

"I think we might," said Papa. "Eh, Susannah?"

"You can come in our car," said Daniel.

"Well! So happy to meet you," said Mrs. Rider helping Isaac Barrey into the car. "I don't imagine you remember my husband very well—Bruce Rider?"

"Not at all," said Papa cheerfully. "I forgot that Lynn and Ben had any kids at all. But then, that's my age telling."

Susan and Daniel sat on either side of the old man. Daniel rolled down his window. "Mmm, smell," he said. "All the rotting leaves from last fall. Thawed out. It smells so rich and garbagy."

"Smells *strong*," said Papa. "Like coffee. I like strong smells like coffee. Weak ones my nose won't even notice anymore."

The house, filled with people, got warm. Someone opened the door, and a warm wind came rolling in from the lake. Daniel was kept busy tossing people's coats on his parents' bed. Where were the Myer House people?

Susan met Daniel on the stairs. "Daniel, wait," she said, interrupting him in mid-lunge. "I want to tell you something."

"What?"

"Don't you think it's strange that Papa's here tonight? That he came out to have dinner with your family when he doesn't even know you?"

"Well—yeah, I guess so."

"He hardly ever goes out, except to church. But he told me today why he wanted to come." Susan's eyes were wide. "He said he had a dream about you the other night."

Daniel stared.

"He said he didn't even remember your grandparents that well, but he dreamed of you, distinctly. He dreamed you were there in the orchard, watching him go by on Mr. Grober's snowmobile."

Daniel sat down on a step. "Oh, wow. I wonder if that means Jason dreamed me, too."

"You can ask him yourself. He's in your kitchen looking for some ice cubes."

"And Alma—would Alma have dreamed of me?"

"Alma couldn't have—she's dead. She never even met you. Never even heard of you," said Susan.

"Yeah, but dreams are wide," said Daniel.

"We're here," cried the voice of Father Marston.

Daniel leaped up. August?

Father Marston sailed into the hall, carrying a covered dish. "There's our favorite," he called out to Daniel. "And Miss Barrey! What a pleasure." He was in good spirits. He took off his coat. Sam Phalen came in, and then— Martha Phalen, with a gaunt Nikos on her arm. No Father August Petrakis.

"I know you're looking for August, but he's not home yet," said Father Marston, helping Martha off with her coat. "Any day now, Daniel, and if he's not back to help me with the Easter Sunday services, I'll make short work of him."

"But he's supposed to be back by tomorrow!" cried Daniel.

"Yes, but you know August." Father Marston grinned. "Between the two of us, if he shows up on time it'll be an accident."

"Between the dozens of us, Father Marston," said Martha. "Father August is renowned for his lapses. I bet he was late for his own ordination."

"You want to take our coats, Daniel, it'll help to pass the time," said Father Marston. He gently helped Nikos off with his jacket and handed it to Daniel.

"Hello, Nikos," said Daniel. Nikos wore his usual unblinking, uncomprehending expression. Martha Phalen guided him into the bright, noisy living room. Daniel bounded back up the stairs with the new armload of coats.

When he came down, his mother was arranging the dishes that people had brought. "Oh, I'm no good at this," she said. A geometric design made of platters and silver and Pyrex casseroles ornamented the dining-room table.

"It looks okay," said Daniel. "Did you meet Nikos, Mommy?"

His mother paused with a battery of serving utensils in her hand. "I can't exactly say. I introduced myself. I'm not sure, though, that I met him, or he me."

"What did you think?"

"Daniel, I've only seen him for a few seconds." She set spoons and big silver forks next to the main courses. "Actually, he looked drunk to me."

"Mommy."

"I know, I know, but you asked me. That's not to say he is. I do hope he enjoys himself. Now, Daniel, tell your father to announce that everything's ready to eat."

"I heard that," said Jason Meister, "and I'm ready to eat, too. It all looks wonderful."

"Certainly does." Vera bobbed her head vigorously. "And it sure is nice to be at a party back in this house again, Marion. How I've missed it."

The crowd came in slowly. Daniel and Susan went into the vacated living room for a few minutes. Nikos was sitting on the piano bench.

"Can I get you anything?" said Susan.

After a while Daniel said, "Can you play the piano, Nikos?"

Nikos just sat.

"Oh, come on," said Daniel. He shook Nikos's shoulder. "Are you in there? Hello?"

"Daniel, stop," said Susan.

Nikos blinked and looked at Daniel. His lips parted. "Mark?"

"This is like a bad dream," said Susan. "I hope that your Father August gets back soon. Let's go get some supper."

"We might as well."

Conversations and aromas threaded the air. "Rats," said Daniel, "all the meatballs are gone." He grabbed a plate and started on the buffet route, squeezing past people who were standing too close to the table. Susan followed eagerly. The voices provided intriguing backdrop as they forked sliced meat and ladled soup and dripped salad dressing and tore desperately at the bread, which had the consistency of not-yet-dried asphalt.

"Just a thaw. We'll have another big storm yet," said Sam Phalen. "The whole winter's been about six weeks late this year. This that we're experiencing just now is the January thaw, I bet."

"Rubbish. This is it. A mild winter that's now over," said someone else. "The ice on the lake'll go before the week's out."

"I suppose it's just a matter of time before I call a lawyer," said Father Marston. "I've tried talking to him, but he's just not responsive. I can't even get him to sign checks so that I can pay his bills out of his account. I've covered the urgent ones myself, but of course I can't do that forever."

"He looked like a little boy," boomed Jason's undampered voice. "A little heap of clothes and bones on the ice. I picked him up—he weighs a good deal less than some cartons I've had to haul in my day—and all he would say was 'Lights, lights.' I thought he was blinded, since he didn't seem to see me."

"He doesn't seem to see anyone," said Mrs. Phalen.

"Oh, do you think so?" said Mrs. Rider happily. "I'm so glad you like it. To me, it seems a bit—well, resilient—but then I lose perspective, baking all the time."

"Tasty," swore Vera, chewing with good will.

"Just finished a bookcase in his room," said Sam. "Got the last coat of paint on it last night. Though why I was hurrying I can't tell you. He'll miss his plane or he'll lose track of time—"

"Or he'll have forgotten he ever lived anyplace else," interrupted Martha, and everyone laughed.

Daniel scooped up an extra plate of food and brought it into the living room. Nikos was still sitting on the piano bench. "A little supper," said Daniel, and set the plate down next to him.

"Don't you want anything?" Daniel picked up a celery stick crammed with creamed cheese, and brought it to Nikos's face. "See? It's good."

"Daniel, don't, that's disgusting," said Susan. "You're talking to him like he was a baby."

"Oh." It was true, and Daniel was ashamed.

The crowd began to surge back into the living room. To escape, Daniel and Susan carried their plates out to the sun porch, which was a little room off the living room, enclosed with three walls of windows. Daniel pushed aside someone's pocketbook and sat down on the edge of the sloping sofa. The television had been moved out here to make room for more chairs in the living room, and it was turned on. A tremendous swordfight was being enacted.

Before long, Daniel and Susan were entranced. "What is this, anyway?" said Daniel.

"Something old—I think I've seen it before," said Susan. "Something like *Hamlet* or something."

At the commercial, Susan scrambled for the program guide, under a heap of the Sunday *New York Times*. Daniel tried to adjust the reception. He never knew what he was doing at those knobs, but he always fooled around with them anyway. It made him feel like his father.

A shadow over him made him turn around. It was Nikos, stiff as a cigar-store Indian, standing at the door.

"Hiding from the crowds, eh," said Daniel. "Sit down on the couch. We're watching something with sword-fights."

"*Romeo and Juliet*," announced Susan.

"Oh, yuck," said Daniel. But he didn't turn it off.

"No wonder it looked familiar," said Susan. "I saw this down in Miami last year with some friends. I remember the balcony scene, and all the beautiful costumes."

"I don't know how we're supposed to understand it," said Daniel. "All in that old English."

"Shut up and listen," said Susan.

They stared. The gray image from the screen seemed

just the distillation of the pressing warm night on the
wide windows, like night brought indoors and rendered
comprehensible, in a box.

"Ugh," said Daniel. "Another dead one. They're dropping like flies. I thought violence on television was on its
way out?"

"Shut UP," said Susan calmly.

The television movie was like a spell. Daniel forgot to
go back for seconds on food. Susan was mesmerized. Even
Nikos sat forward on the couch, thin elbows leaning on
knobby knees, and seemed to be watching.

For I have need of many orisons
To move the heavens to smile upon my state,
Which, well thou know'st, is cross and full of sin.

"Daniel," called his mother, above the noise of the
party.

"Oh, not now," complained Daniel.

"I heard that. Come here, please."

Juliet was about to take some kind of medicine that
would make her look as if she were dead. She was going
to be carried to the tomb. Then Romeo would meet her
at the tomb, and she would wake up and not really be
dead, and they would be together, and run away from all
the swordfighting and violence and snarling parents.

"Just a minute, Mommy," Daniel called.

"No. I need you, Daniel."

"It's *educational!*"

But there was no disobeying his father's stern "Daniel."

He ran from the sun porch. "Would you carry these cups of coffee to the people in the living room, please, Daniel?" said his mother. "I'm busy in the kitchen, washing spoons."

Daniel picked up two cups of coffee and twisted toward the door.

"Gently," said his father.

He was on his way back to get the next two cups when Jason Meister thundered, "Well, look who's here!"

Daniel abandoned his chore and tried to see around Jason's barricading bulk.

"Welcome back, Father," cried Vera Meister. "On schedule and everything."

It was he, it was Father August Petrakis, grinning like a boy and throwing his head back. The warm night blew in around him. "I saw on the calendar where everyone was meeting, so how could I stay away?" he said.

Daniel, in the back of the crowd, felt as if he were seeing August for the first time. Grabbing the cigarettes and matches out of his pockets before someone took away his coat, August looked thin, concentrated, durable. He looked like himself. That was enough to make Daniel glad. I'm not mad at you, I'm not, he chanted voicelessly across the room. Look at me.

"Coffee?" said Mrs. Rider.

"Brother returned to the fold!" said Father Marston, hugging him.

Daniel had moved to the stairs for a better look, and August saw him standing there. He winked, and Daniel was suffused with relief. The welcoming parishioners wanted to hear all about New Mexico and the monastery there. August winked at Daniel again and rolled his eyes. "Let me wash up first," he protested, and then he was charging up the stairs.

Daniel reached out his hand. August caught it and pulled Daniel upstairs behind him. "Friend," said August, lighting a cigarette in the shadows of the upstairs hall, "speak to me."

"Welcome home," said Daniel, feeling stupid and inarticulate and happy.

"Ah, but I haven't been away," said August. He ducked into the bathroom to flick the burnt match into the toilet, and came back and drew on his cigarette. "I'll see you soon, and you'll tell me everything; encapsulate for now. How are you? You look tired."

"I'm okay. It's not me—" Nikos was in the forefront of Daniel's concerns, but he remembered suddenly the feeling of being unimportant, left behind, when August had gone away; the feeling came to him vividly and he didn't know what to say.

"You look as if you're all tied in knots."

Daniel opened his mouth and a scream sounded, but it wasn't Daniel's voice. It came from the sun porch. "Don't do it! Don't! She's not really dead! She's only sleeping!"

"God in heaven, what's that?" groaned August. "Trauma in the opening five minutes. This play moves fast." He stuck the cigarette in his mouth and put his hand on Daniel's neck for a second. "Keep it hot, I'll be right back." And then he hurried down the stairs.

Daniel followed. There was a great wailing from the sun porch.

"That sounds like—" said August, and he pushed through the people crowded at the door. Daniel kept close behind him.

Susan was standing at the television. The white dot was still dwindling; she must have just turned the set off. "Romeo was about to kill himself when he found Juliet dead, only she was sleeping really, and Nikos—"

"Nick!" said August.

Nikos was on his hands and knees; a wild look flashed in his eye. "She's not really dead, don't do it," he said.

"I didn't even have a chance to tell you," began Father Marston.

"Nick," said Father August, and he was down on his knees next to Nikos, pulling him upright, steadying the shivering face between his palms. "Nick Griskas! What in the name of God are you carrying on about?"

Nikos looked at August and tears flowed. His mouth opened and his lips moved, but words were slow in coming. Just one rose up from the depths of him. It balanced on his lips and fell hopelessly into the room; he looked intently at August as he spoke.

"Mark?" he said.

Again, it was sound first, and the sound kept thumping until it married an image, and the image's wings were broad and its eyes bright.

Stirred from sleep, Daniel pulled himself to the window.

"Why don't you just fly in?" he murmured unhappily, having been awoken from a sad part of sleep. "You can navigate through glass all the other times." Daniel could just refuse to open the window, if he decided that, and the bird would go away.

But it was too close to danger, the mist pushing forward and Nikos falling back, and everywhere in the melting world the skin of ice cracking. Daniel threw open the window.

The bird circled. Daniel pulled on a pair of his father's socks (he'd borrowed them just for this occasion). They came up to his knees. Then he flew after the dark bird.

Perhaps it was because he was so recently awake that the world seemed to be shuddering. Trees shook and limbfuls of snow and ice thudded to the muddy ground. The nearer slopes and the lawns and banks ran with a thin varnish of water. From his vantage point Daniel could see that the ice on Canaan Lake was no longer a seal, a lock, but was instead an island, a flat island, separated on all sides from the shore by a few feet of dark water.

They drifted high along the margin of the lake, through belts of warmer and then cooler wind. Daniel felt like a kite.

And he descended like a kite, when it was time to descend: resisting. This flying was beginning to delight him, and the dream would no doubt confuse him. Daniel balked a bit. But the bird swam on in the warm currents, and there was no way to fly without him. So Daniel swam on.

In a narrowing spiral they flew. A broad expanse of roof showed among the lakeside trees. It was a few minutes before Daniel recognized it as the Myer House, with the new chapel built onto one end and the kitchen garden behind a wall on the other. August's dream, wondered Daniel. Or Martha's, or Sam's, or Father Marston's?

The bird altered its course and swept a wide circle out over the lake, Daniel following, of course. Wheeling like a couple of summer barn swallows, they dipped and swung and banked left over the ice, and turned to the shore again. The boathouse, its yawning doorway offering dark haven, and its windows above just black squares, sat on its manmade pilings, a causeway's reach from the mainland, a lookout over the lake. Into one of its dark windows on the second floor the bird and Daniel flew.

There was only an instant's recognition of the blanketed sleeper: Nikos in dream. And the dream swept up like a hot wind around Daniel, not waiting for welcome.

Papa's dream had been spartan and slow; Jason's was rich, brassy. But if Jason's was a carnival, Nikos's dream was a maelstrom.

Oranges. A horse. A verdant moonlit lawn. A snatch of symphonic music, trailing off in the wind. A woman with soft hands. A childhood birthday with tin soldiers marching about on a flagstoned walk. Lights, darkness, lights again.

The bird settled on Daniel's shoulder. It opened its mouth. Though Daniel could hear no sound, perhaps its unimaginable voice was the force that called the dream to order, or to a semblance of order.

Nikos was on a balcony in Ierapetra, on the island of Crete. It was a velvety, chilly October night. A bottle of Metaxa stood on the rail, and a moon spied down on him. Nikos sipped from his glass and wrote a letter. "When I get home," he wrote, "let's take a trip somewhere. Go camping. Maybe up in the Adirondacks." The wind of the Mediterranean rippled the paper Nikos wrote on. An old blind fiddler began to play in the shadows of a doorway down in the street.

Greece disappeared, the winds, the luminous buildings in the moonlight, the Metaxa, and the letter. The fiddler kept playing.

Nikos was on a forested slope, and the night broke harsh threats in the woods around him. He was looking for the tent where he'd left Mark. The trees lifted their black grillwork, an impenetrable, delicate prison around him. The cold rammed at him like a brute. His boots were filled with snow and his feet slowly freezing. He had to get back to the camp.

Filoretti, a girl with magical black hair, came into the kitchen. Come outside and make a snowman with me, Nick, she said. Here, I'll help you put on your boots. No, said Nick, I don't want to. I want to stay here and be warm. I'm drawing a picture, see? Filoretti didn't look.

On ice, polished like a ballroom floor, Nikos ran, toward

the lights and the mist and the columns. The night fragmented with Nikos's desperation. But the lights would not absorb Nikos. The key was missing.

Nikos was in the woods. Just beyond the trees was the tent. He could see it. He could see inside it, but he could not get there. Mark was dying. Wait for me, Nikos called. He struggled through the bracken.

The fire in front of the tent was out. The smoke tapered into hands. The hands drifted to Nikos and clamped themselves on his ankles and wrists; he couldn't move.

Mark went away. Nikos was bound.

On a lawn, Mark lay on his back in a gully. Over on the edge of the lawn apparent guests mingled and chattered. The sounds of laughing and clinking forks tumbled forth. The guests were two-dimensional, like a frieze, moving but shadowy.

You can't stay here, said Mark kindly.

I can't leave, said Nikos, on his knees. I'm bound.

But I'm dead, said Mark.

The funeral picnic noise stilled. The guests were waiting for Nikos to come back to them.

Filoretti descended from the upper bunk, waking Nikos with a kick. She showed him the stocking at the end of the bed, lumpy with an orange and crayons and raisins and seven tin soldiers. But where did this come from? cried Nikos, bouncing up and down, hitting his head on the springs of the upper bunk. Everything today is a present, said Filoretti solemnly, unwrapping a chocolate Santa. Come on, let's go see if it snowed out.

Juliet pulled on big white mittens and said to her nurse, Come on, let's go, he's waiting. It's too cold, said the nurse, you'll never get out of Verona today, the highway authorities have issued travelers' advisories.

Nikos was in a bathroom, spitting toothpaste in a sink. There was a skylight overhead, and the full moon glowed orange through the glass. Nikos turned, rested on the edge of the sink, and looked up. Suppose you come back, he thought, and the world has torn through space, and the earth is not where it was in the skies, how will you find me? Nikos stood on the toilet and tried to open the skylight, in case he was coming back. But the ice clamped the window shut.

Come on, said Filoretti, dancing in her school clothes. Let's bundle up and go build a snow fort.

No, said Nikos. I never wanted to before and I don't now either. I have a death on my hands, and hands on my death, and a debt in my breast, and breath still.

The fiddler from Ierapetra closed his tune.

Filoretti, wounded, went off and got married.

The moon dwindled to a white dot and vanished.

Nikos stared at the ground. Mark was gone. The guests were growing dimmer. The hands at his ankles and wrists, the strong fingers of guilt, tightened.

He sat down and waited to freeze.

Daniel felt frozen himself. It was only the bird's insistent wings that disengaged him from the frozen dream. The bird flew several times around Daniel, as if wrapping invisible cords of warmth around him, and then began its return flight.

Daniel was led, unthinking, back to his bedroom, and he slept till dawn, dreamless.

Chapter Fourteen

Now that Father August was back, the first thing to be done was to take the feather and show it to him, and see what he thought. This was no time for petty grudges and hurt feelings.

"First plans of the day," said Mrs. Rider, "include vacuuming the front rooms of party crumbs."

"Oh, Ma," said Daniel.

"You heard me. Faster you get started, faster you'll finish."

"But I wanted to go to the Myer House—"

"Daniel, it's Good Friday," said Mrs. Rider. "Not really a day for socializing. I think you should plan to spend a quiet time this afternoon. If you want to go to Stations at the chapel with me, you're welcome. But I'd rather you didn't gallivant around."

Daniel pounded up to his room in anger.

In fact, he was angry about everything. That impossible flying to those indecipherable dreams—what was it all for? Where was it getting him? What should he be doing about it?

Jason, Papa, Nikos—what was the link? Why had the

bird, born of mist, led him to those dreams? Daniel knew there must be a reason. But the reason escaped him.

He took out his notebook and began to write.

Mrs. Rider came in the room with a change of sheets. "What are you working on?"

"I don't know," said Daniel. "I'm just sort of scribbling, trying to figure things out. All these dead people in our lives."

"You mean Grandma?"

"Or anyone. There's lots more people dead than alive. Everyone knows someone who's dead. How can you keep from caring about them?"

"You can't." Mrs. Rider began stripping Daniel's bed, though it was a job he usually did for himself. "You're thinking about your father and your grandmother, aren't you?"

Daniel didn't say.

Mrs. Rider sat down suddenly on the bare mattress, the sheets twisted in her hands. "You can't judge everything at face value, Daniel. It's been very hard on your father to move back here surrounded by his mother's things, every minute of it a reminder of her and her life that's gone now. But he was willing to do it because my doctors recommended the move out of the city for me—a characteristically loving gesture without any of the sentimental words about it. Don't you think it was hard for him to leave the city? But it was the best thing for my health and I haven't heard him complain for one minute. It's not that he's blasé about the death of his mother—in fact, I think he misses her a great deal—but he cares about us more. It shows in his actions. You have to learn to read a person's actions as well as his words."

Daniel turned. "He hasn't cared about Grandma's things being thrown to the four winds. He hasn't cared—"

"There's caring and there's *caring*," said Mrs. Rider, swooping with a kiss down to Daniel's forehead, trailing sheets. "It's a matter of learning the language. And it's never easy. Incidentally, what are you doing with that old painting? I thought I'd set that aside for your father to decide about."

The *Blizzard of '88* stood on Daniel's desk. "He'd just throw it out. You know that."

"If you want it, ask him for it," said Mrs. Rider. "That's an order."

At one-thirty Mrs. Rider and Daniel got in the car. The day was being scrubbed by a strong east wind; a cleanliness and submerged warmth was returning to the world. The sky was baroque with cream-and-ocher clouds massively billowing in the silky blue.

And everywhere, ice melted.

"Won't be long before budding," said Mrs. Rider. "And then all this clear moonlike space will be filled up and hidden by green. I wish I'd been here to plant a few daffodils last fall."

Daniel touched the feather in his pocket.

Susan met him at the chapel door. Papa was safely settled up near the front, where he could hear.

"Father Marston said that Father August is supposed to
help with the service," Susan said.

"Well, let's go find him, before it starts," said Daniel.
They ran in the front door of the Myer House and
clattered up the stairs.

"Hold your horses," said Martha Phalen from the kitchen. "You just don't run in and out of here like this was
a gymnasium. Besides, Father August is out in the boathouse with Nikos. You'd better tell him that the service
starts in about five minutes."

"Thanks. Sorry," yelled Daniel, and away they ran,
down the path along the causeway and up the stairs to the
second-floor room. This time Daniel knocked.

"Come in," called August.

They entered in silence. August was sitting on a coffee
table, and Nikos was still on the sofa, covered with
blankets, in the same position Daniel had seen him in last
night. August finished a cigarette and rubbed it out.

"Bearers of hope," he said, "speak to me. I'm ready to
go up in a puff of smoke."

"What's wrong?" said Daniel.

"My friend Nikos Griskas. I think he's at the end."
August shivered and ran a hand through his dark hair.
"I'm about to call for a doctor. Or run get my oils."

Then he sat up and tried to smile. "Some welcome I've
given you. Tell me something good."

"Mrs. Phalen said to tell you the services were about to start," said Susan.

"Oh, the time!" August clapped a palm to his forehead and started to rise. "I should be over at chapel—all vested and ready—"

Daniel had taken the feather from his coat pocket. He stood with it gingerly in his hands, like a ring bearer at a wedding.

August stopped in mid-speech. His eyes blazed. Susan and Daniel were frightened for a minute; what had descended on him? When he spoke—"Where did you get that?"— his voice was unusually soft.

"From a bird," said Daniel, "who came out of a cloud."

August reached for the feather and held it close to his eyes, and then closed his eyes and weighed it in his hands.

"This is not ours," he said at last, "not ours at all. Not in this world. Daniel, Susan, start at the beginning and tell me everything."

Daniel, the chronicler, spoke. Susan nodded agreement. Because Nikos seemed insensible to the telling, Daniel offered liberal descriptions of Nikos's confusion and the mystery of the dreams.

"And that's all it's about," he finished, "and it doesn't make much sense to me: fog and sorrow, and sorrow and mist, and dreams I don't understand."

August didn't say anything for a minute. He turned and stared out the boathouse windows, across the watery ice.

Daniel waited. Susan waited. The sun caught on the

glass and warmed Daniel's neck. From away in the chapel the labored singing of the congregation sounded. Whoops, thought Daniel, Mommy will kill me for skipping the service. He looked at the water.

"Oh," he said calmly, "the lights."

In the full brilliance of day the lights on the lake had arisen, burning furious, slow implosions of some light other than daylight, lining up into the columns, the pillars throbbing into the day . . .

. . . and time was held still, the hands of the clock ceased their navigation. Even the voices of the choir were holding one note through the timelessness.

"Why wasn't I here?" August looked excited and puzzled; he scratched his head and squinted at Daniel. "Why when I went away? But the feather, it's not meant to stay here. It should go back before the lights burn any brighter. Who could say what would happen?" The feather flipped from his fingers, darted like a paper airplane, fluttered, and landed on the blanket covering Nikos.

Daniel grabbed the feather.

"Time to think," said August, speaking more to himself than to them. "Who can say what would happen if the lights burned right into the day?"

"There's no time," said Daniel, trying to help. "Time's stopped."

"No time." August looked as if he was adding long columns of figures in his head, concentrating fiercely. "I think I should bring it back," he said finally.

"Why you?" said Susan.

"Because I don't know what will happen," said August. "Give it to me."

"Happen? To you?" Daniel felt a chill pinch his spine. "What do you mean, happen?"

"I don't know what I mean," said August in an even voice, "but I don't think there's much time."

"There's *no* time. I told you that already," said Daniel irritably. "You can't just walk into the lights, August. We don't even know what they are."

"You should have called me," said the priest.

"You didn't leave a number. You didn't leave any address," said Susan, as usual the one to speak right out. "You didn't even pay much attention to Daniel when he ran all the way from school to say goodbye before you left. Why should he have called you?"

"I didn't want you to miss me too much," said August, looking at Daniel. "I didn't want you to neglect making other friends in favor of me, who was far away."

"Well, of *course* I missed you," said Daniel.

"But he made a friend anyway," said Susan loyally, and in case anyone was uncertain, she added, "Me."

August looked at Daniel, at Susan, at Nikos. "I didn't mean to hurt you," he said to Daniel. "I'm sorry about that."

"Well, don't go talking about taking the stupid feather back," said Daniel, "especially if you think there's any danger."

"Besides," said Susan, "it's Daniel's feather, not yours."

August said calmly, "I don't think we should wait very much longer. Give it to me, Daniel."

But Susan said, "It's not up to you, August. This is Daniel's whole mess. Daniel's the one who had the dreams. I even took the damn feather and I didn't have any dreams. The bird came out over the water looking for someone and Daniel was the one he chose. So it's up to him."

Daniel said, "The dreams were mine. I didn't ask for them. If the bird had come to Nikos, maybe he'd have spoken in poetry, or in something Nikos could understand—if he'd come to you, maybe visions or something. But for me it was dreams, August, and all of them had reaching in them, leaning across; I told you about them, Jason reaching for Alma, old Isaac for his baby boy, Nikos reaching for Mark." Daniel swallowed and tried hard to put into words the thoughts that were just now being born in his mind. "I think that the feather wasn't really mine at all. I think it was for Nikos. All those dreams were about death, and Nikos is the one so sick over death. I think I was only holding it for him."

"Are you sure?" said August.

"No," said Daniel. "But it's the only thing I can figure out right now."

"Then if the feather has to go back, Nikos should bring it back," said Susan.

"Not on your life," said August.

"It's *his* life," said Susan, getting excited, "and there's not much of it evident right now, is there?"

August said, "I forbid it," and Daniel at the same time said, "She's right, I think she's right—Nikos should take it back—"

"I'll take him, then," said August, "but for crying out loud, I'm going right now. There's no time—"

"Right. No time," said Daniel, slipping an arm around Nikos. "And it was my dreams, so I'm going too."

"And I didn't have the feather or any dreams, but just try and stop me," said Susan, getting on the other side of Nikos.

August stared at them, struggling with Nikos, who was far too unwieldy for them to carry alone, and then he shrugged, his shoulders hunched, his palms opened up and uplifted as if checking for rain, and he let out a long relieved laugh and said, "Well, we'd better get going, then."

Susan and August tugged at an aluminum rowboat that had been stored against an inner wall of the boathouse. The gloom and damp of the boat room was lit, though, with a luminousness frightening in its intensity. Daniel, supporting Nikos at the door, was blinded; the light seemed to emanate from everything, as if the boats, the orange, mildewy life jackets, the oars and paddles and green coils of rope were, for once, dispensing original light rather than reflecting some parent light. The full grimy substance of things shone.

"The ice won't hold," Susan huffed, "so we'll take a boat and break it as we go."

"And give back the feather before it's too late, before the apocalypse thunders," said August, and he continued muttering wildly to himself about time and being and grace and salvation. He seemed to lose realization that the children and Nikos were helping him drop the aluminum rowboat into the electric water, that they were, all of them, scrambling in and tussling with oars and trying to move the boat out of the stone-and-clapboard harbor into the brilliant ice of the lake.

"Look out," said Daniel, stepping on August's foot to get to the prow of the rowboat.

"What are you doing?" said Susan.

"Breaking the ice," said Daniel, because he knew how.

He held up the feather, and the boat began to move. They never had to touch the oars. Calm Susan Barrey and apprehensive Father August Petrakis and wild-eyed Nikos Griskas and uncomprehending Daniel Rider, all riders in the lightweight craft, all pulled slowly through steaming waters by one uplifted feather.

The ice sank. As the boat glided along, the ice around it simply sank, and the lakewater lapped gently at the sides of the boat.

Far back on the shore, the choir sustained their note, and as its sound faded—because the boat was drawing away from it—a sense of inevitability replaced the urgency of the mission.

The lights on the lake, the shining mists, were assembled and steady, and slowly, slowly, the southeast shore of Canaan Lake was lost, and the Adirondack mountains were lost, and the pungent odors of trees and lakewater and ice and mud and fish were lost. The boat moved forward toward the lights, but the rest of the world was unraveled and dissembled. There was only an aluminum rowboat with four dazed passengers skimming on the water.

The mist warmed them. Daniel felt no tiredness at having to hold aloft the feather.

"We're crossing some water wider than Canaan Lake," said Susan. "We should have reached my side of the lake by now."

"The transitus," said August.

On they went.

On they went.

Have I ever done anything else, ever, but ride in a rowboat toward the lights, Daniel wondered once.

On they went.

The boat slows.

They wake up. They look up. A bird of all brightness hovers not far from them. It opens its mouth and calls in an unutterable voice, and the feather leaves Daniel's hand and melds back into the bird.

There is an unbearable, unending explosion of light,

and through it the shapes that had been pillars and stripes move slowly. Daniel stares, knowing he must be being blinded.

The closest form moves a little closer and seems to smile.

Mark, says Nikos, without surprise.

The form—the person—Mark—released from the mist, holds out his hands.

You can't stay, says Mark. You belong in time.

Nikos steps past Susan, August, Daniel. Forgive me, Mark, he says, crying.

But you don't need forgiveness, says Mark.

Forgive me, says Nikos, bending.

Their hands touch, Nikos in the boat and Mark in the mist, their four hands clasp. I forgive you, then, says Mark.

Nikos sinks down into the laps of Susan and Father August. Already Mark is being recovered by the lights. For a moment the lights shine, and a music that exists without the structure of time sings, and a host of the dead are there. Daniel almost thinks that he sees his grandmother, off to one side, but not too far.

The boat, without the feather now, begins of its own accord to slowly drift back. By gravity, it returns to its birth time and place.

The lights on the lake begin to fade.

And, like infants being rocked, the four travelers sleep.

Nikos didn't wake.

August and Daniel were pulling on the oars, hoisting the aluminum rowboat over the ice-free lake, and Susan was trailing her fingers in the water. "I'll need another retreat, a permanent one," said August happily, "in order to understand this."

"Listen," said Daniel. "You can still hear the choir."

They put up the oars, stilled the dripping, and listened. The world around them was perfectly still. Even the clouds were motionless.

The last of the shining mists was fading. The solid angles of the Grobers' house and the stone Barrey house began to show through. They all savored the last bit of perfect stillness—

—and then the lights were gone, and the choir wheezed along to the next verse.

"Come on," said August, laughing, "we can still catch the benediction if we hurry."

"We'll have to carry Nikos up," said Susan, "as he doesn't seem to be waking."

Chapter Fifteen

O n Saturday, in the late afternoon, Daniel found
Father August and Father Marston and Martha Phalen
arranging the big vases of lilies in the chapel. "The vigil
service will be here, and then Sam will have to truck the
flowers over to St. Mark's for the Easter Sunday services,"
explained Father Marston. "Complicated business."

"You're crowding your side together, Father Marston,"
said Martha Phalen, standing back. "Give them a little
more room."

"Give *me* a little more room, this is like a greenhouse
up here," Father Marston complained.

Daniel fingered some slender candles lined up in a
cardboard box. "What're these for?"

"The light service. You remember," said August.

"I've never been to one," said Daniel, "I don't think."

"Oh, it's great, come tonight," said August. "All the
lights are turned out, and then the Paschal candle is lit
and carried from the doors up to the altar. And everyone
holds a candle, and the light is passed from the Paschal
candle to everyone's candle, till the whole place is ablaze
with shared light."

The place was ablaze already, with strengthening sunlight on the snow-white lilies. Mrs. Phalen took a rag to the stack of red hymnals and vigorously dusted. "You fathers better get those announcements out to the lectern before the choir arrives to warm up, or they'll keep you talking all afternoon."

"Stay for supper," said August, "and then you can stay for the vigil service at eight-thirty."

"I'll call home and see," said Daniel.

"That urchin at our table again?" said Martha Phalen. "We might as well give him his own room and charge him top dollar for room and board." Daniel grinned and went to call his mother.

"A light dinner tonight," said Martha Phalen, setting a vegetable casserole on the table. "Tomorrow we'll feast."

Father Marston offered a grace, and they all sat down.

"With all the commotion about Nikos, we haven't had a chance to hear about your trip," said Sam Phalen. "Successful?"

"Great," said Father August.

"What wouldn't I give for six weeks in the desert," said Martha Phalen. "I'd put on my fluffy pink slippers and never give a second thought to all that dust blowing around. Daniel, help yourself to milk if you want it."

"I could use six weeks away, to rest up from the effort of doing all the Lenten programs and services without you," said Father Marston. "Now if I could just persuade the Bishop to finance me—but I'd rather the Riviera than New Mexico."

"I'm glad to be back, though," said August. "And, all of you, I'm grateful for your taking care of Nikos. I know it must have been a trial."

"Well, Daniel came and visited him often," said Martha. She piled seconds on Daniel's plate without asking if he wanted them. "He may have many faults but he's a loyal friend."

"Hear, hear," said August, lifting his water glass in a toast.

"An hour till the service begins," said Father Marston, at the end of the meal. "This time, dear Father Petrakis, please don't be late."

"On my honor," said August.

"No, don't bother with the dishes, Sam and I'll get them," Martha was saying when Nikos appeared at the doorway.

"Aha," said Father Marston tentatively, "you're awake."

"And ravenous," said Nikos, in a clear voice that Daniel had never heard before. "Maybe I could snitch a little of that leftover casserole before it goes back to the kitchen?"

"You sit right down there, young man, and I'll heat it up so it's edible," cried Martha Phalen, "and it's about time, too."

"Welcome back," said Father August, an uncontrollable smile sounding through his voice. "I thought you might not wake up."

"I've slept long enough," said Nikos, "though not without my share of dreams." He tilted his head and looked at

Daniel. "I know you from somewhere—I dreamed about you."

"My good friend Daniel Rider," said August.

"Well, hello," said Nikos to Daniel, and to the salad Martha had brought in and set down before him. "Don't mind if I just go ahead—"

"Good to have you back, Nick," said August. "I'll talk to you after the vigil service."

"I'll be there," promised Nikos through a mouthful of lettuce. "I've got to call my sister first, though, and find out how things are."

August was taking an hour of prayer before the service began, so Daniel put on his blue coat and white scarf and went out for a walk.

The winter stars, a thousand points of light, glittered like snow. Daniel longed for the feather and the bird, so he could fly up over the thawed lake, closer to the Dippers and friendly Orion, closer to the wind. And into some-one's dream again . . .

He hadn't yet begun to understand what had happened yesterday, when the luminous Mark Nesbitt had blessed and forgiven Nikos. August had proved little help. "Write it down," he said, "and think about it for yourself. I use words that mean the world to me, but I don't want to muddle you up."

"But how could Mark speak if he's dead?" Daniel protested.

"It was Mark's friendship speaking," said August

slowly. "We are caught in a chain of days, Daniel, from which we can't escape. We're on a train in time, from being born to being dead, but the things that happen to us in our lives accumulate us, multiply us in ourselves. Once out of time, Daniel, we shine. Oh, I'm messing it up for you, I can see that. Just write it down as you saw it, and it'll make sense eventually."

So Daniel had written it down in his notebook last night, and he thought about it tonight, as he stood on the muddy ridge at the edge of the lake.

If something happened once, it happens always, August had said.

For a long time Daniel watched the lake, half expecting an unfolding of mists and lights. But only the dark shore and scattered light from houses showed, only what belonged there.

No mist. No bird.

Suppose Susan was right. Suppose the bird had come out of the mist looking for someone to lead through some dreams, to help bring Nikos to that unearthly meeting; why hadn't the bird picked someone else? Susan, or Ed Gourney, or any other of the townspeople of Canaan Lake? Why him?

Was it because he'd felt so lonely himself this past six weeks that the bird had come to him? Had the bird known that Daniel sometimes felt as alone as Nikos had, and so would sympathize with him, befriend him?

Or maybe, he thought, it's simpler than that. Maybe the bird came to me because it knew I'd be willing to fly after it in the night without kicking up a fuss. Can't imagine Martha Phalen soaring through the night sky without knowing where she was headed!

Still, Daniel wished the bird would come back, and he knew it never would.

Cars began pulling into the driveway and parking, and people hobbled on good shoes and splashed in the puddles as they headed toward the chapel.

I really will have to try to read some more of Nikos's poetry, Daniel thought; maybe now I'll understand some of it.

"Daniel, come here." His mother was hurrying toward him with sheet music tucked under her arm and a platter between her white-gloved hands. "Will you take this cake in to Mrs. Phalen? I may still be an amateur when it comes to bread, but my Easter cake has never been excelled. Thanks, I'm late for warm-up already."

"Where's Daddy?"

"Home painting the bathroom. Now, will you want a ride back with me after the service?"

"No, I'll walk." Daniel balanced the platter carefully, so the elegant molded lamb, coconut-fleeced, raisin-eyed, beribboned at the neck, wouldn't slide off into the mud. Mrs. Rider went stalking off toward the chapel.

"What a masterpiece," said Mrs. Phalen in the kitchen. "Make room for it on the top shelf of the refrigerator, Daniel, and then you'd better hurry if you want to get a candle. Sam? Are you ready?"

Daniel went back out into the front yard.

The Grobers from across the lake pulled into the muddy parking lot, bringing Susan and Papa in their car; the old man waved at Daniel and went inside. Jason and Vera pulled up in the delivery truck. Even Ed Gourney was there, with an army of brothers and sisters all older than he.

A lot to look at, thought Daniel. August and Grandma, now and then, are good true friends, but so, too, are Susan Barrey and even Ed Gourney, in his own way. And they'd been willing and waiting all along to be friends, reaching over to him—reaching the way the people in the dreams had been reaching to each other—but Daniel just hadn't seen it.

Susan was standing at the door, beckoning to him, waiting for him.

Nikos ambled over to the chapel and disappeared in the dark doorway, and then Sam and Martha Phalen, he strolling and she urging him faster.

Then Father August, flapping in his white vestments, cleared the stone steps of the Myer House porch and raced to the chapel doors, where Father Marston was prodding the wick of the Paschal candle to make sure it would light.

The night pressed down on him. Daniel moved a couple of feet toward the chapel doors. People with candles stood in shadow, waiting for the light. Susan, impatient, had slipped inside.

Burning off fear, those candles, just as the sun burned early-morning mist off water every warm day, clarifying. All these people who'd stretched out their hands to each other fearlessly, Jason and Alma and Vera, Papa to his son, and Mark and Nikos.

And even his father, hurrying out to hunt for the wandering Nikos that night, despite the inconvenience of it and the resentment he felt about it.

So as the congregation shared their light, Daniel turned and headed for home, thinking: No more dream-flying, but I can at least try by myself. At least I can try. I can ask him if I can have that painting of the Blizzard of '88. I can ask him a lot of things.